Miracle Medics

Now celebrating its fifteenth anniversary,
Dr. David Kennedy's GDK Foundation organizes
a classic car rally through the UK countryside to
raise funds and awareness for transplant surgeries.
It will also give David a chance to
spend some quality time with his adopted son,
Dr. Josh Kennedy, a transplant specialist,
as they work together as navigator and driver.
Or, at least, that *was* the plan…

See classic cars and hearts sent racing as these
medics prove miracles are possible in:

How to Heal the Surgeon's Heart
By Ann McIntosh

As the charity road rally gets underway,
is it the race that has foundation founder
Dr. David Kennedy's heart pounding for the
first time in forever…or is it transplant recipient
coordinator Valerie Sterling?

Risking It All for a Second Chance
By Annie Claydon

When Josh and his ex, Dr. Emma Owen, are forced
to team up to complete the rally, tensions are high
in the confined space of her classic Mini Cooper.
Will the biggest hazard they face be the temptation
to start right where they left off?

Dear Reader,

When the amazing Annie Claydon and I were coming up with the premise for the Miracle Medics duet, we definitely had travel on our minds. We literally started with doctors on a train, then a ship and then, somehow, in cars. In classic cars doing a charity run to raise awareness for the life-saving work transplant teams do.

We had so much fun with the concept, it grew into a fictional event I really wish would happen in real life. My husband, who used to race in both TSD rallies and rally cross, helped hugely when it came to how things work, and Annie and I had a blast figuring out all the details.

I love this concept so much, but my favorite thing was the characters I got to create. An "older" couple, David's committed to his work, and Val's spent so much time taking care of everyone else, she feels a bit lost now that she's on her own. Neither is expecting to find love, and when they do, neither expects it to last.

Here's hoping *How to Heal the Surgeon's Heart* will remind you that love can flower at all ages and stages of life!

Ann McIntosh

HOW TO HEAL
THE SURGEON'S HEART

———

ANN McINTOSH

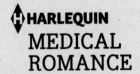

HARLEQUIN

MEDICAL
ROMANCE

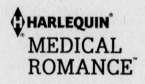

HARLEQUIN®
MEDICAL ROMANCE™

Recycling programs for this product may not exist in your area.

ISBN-13: 978-1-335-40905-8

How to Heal the Surgeon's Heart

This edition published by arrangement with Harlequin Books S.A.

For questions and comments about the quality of this book, please contact us at CustomerService@Harlequin.com.

Harlequin Enterprises ULC
22 Adelaide St. West, 41st Floor
Toronto, Ontario M5H 4E3, Canada
www.Harlequin.com

Printed in U.S.A.

Ann McIntosh was born in the tropics, lived in the frozen north for a number of years and now resides in sunny central Florida with her husband. She's a proud mama to three grown children, loves tea, crafting, animals (except reptiles), bacon and the ocean. She believes in the power of romance to heal, inspire and provide hope in our complex world.

Books by Ann McIntosh

Harlequin Medical Romance

A Summer in São Paulo

Awakened by Her Brooding Brazilian

The Surgeon's One Night to Forever
Surgeon Prince, Cinderella Bride
The Nurse's Christmas Temptation
Best Friend to Doctor Right
Christmas with Her Lost-and-Found Lover
Night Shifts with the Miami Doc
Island Fling with the Surgeon
Christmas Miracle in Jamaica

Visit the Author Profile page at Harlequin.com.

For Mike, who so patiently explained the finer points of rally driving, and who loves me just the way I am, although I don't know a stanchion from a strut!

CHAPTER ONE

DR. DAVID KENNEDY settled into the back of the chauffeur-driven car as it left Liverpool's Lime Street train station and pressed his knuckles against his eyelids for an instant. Then he twisted his head from side to side, trying to ease out the kinks. Beyond the glass, a damp drizzle fell, and the sound of the windshield wipers matched the throbbing in his skull. A tension headache had taken up residence in a band across his forehead, and his eyes were gritty from too little sleep.

Just over three weeks.

That was all the time left before the Rally Round campaign started, and there was so much left to do.

He'd been working nonstop on the logistics—liaising with the rally and classic-car clubs, expanding the events as needed, and drumming up support from news outlets across the UK. Already this morning he'd spoken to his personal assistant three times, answered umpteen emails, and done a radio interview via telephone, all before his eight-fifteen arrival in Liverpool.

That interview had severely tested his patience.

Instead of concentrating on the rally, or even the work of GDK Foundation, the host had wanted to dredge up David's past. Even being adept at deflecting the conversation back to where he wanted it to go hadn't stopped David's temper from rising.

Now, rubbing the back of his neck, he tried to put it behind him, but it stuck in his craw.

Sixteen years was more than enough time for the story to become old news. Yet, nothing he achieved or attempted was enough to divert attention from the past headlines.

Billionaire Financier Dies Leaving Fortune to Son He Never Met

Sir Arthur Knutson's Love Child with Black American Entertainer Inherits

Knutson's Family Sues to Overturn Will

Salacious at the time, with the resulting smear campaigns and court case giving the papers an abundance of trashy headlines, but surely no one was interested anymore?

He was honest enough to admit part of the

problem was his initial decision to capitalize on the unwanted publicity he'd received. It was a plan hatched at one of the lowest, most difficult times of his life. A time when he'd felt he'd lost almost everything he treasured and was desperate to make *some* good come of it.

His mother had once told him, "Davie, always remember this: pick your roles carefully, and then commit to them, completely."

At the time he'd thought she meant it literally, in the show-business sense, so he'd dismissed the advice. Even then he'd been fascinated by science and dreamed of a career in medicine or aeronautics. But, as he'd gotten older, he'd realized her words had far wider applications.

They were words he could live by and did. He carefully chose what he was going to do and, once the choice was made, committed to the plan, fully.

He'd wanted to make a positive difference in other people's lives, which led him to become a doctor. Then, spurred on by the mentorship of one of France's top transplant experts, who was one of his mother's friends, he'd specialized in transplant surgery and risen to the top of his field.

When he'd married Georgie, he'd committed to being the best husband he could be. The best father to her young son too, especially since Josh—like David—didn't know his biological father.

And those decisions had led to what David considered a perfect life.

A normal life, far removed from the glamorous, peripatetic, showbiz one David had grown up in, but lovely in its very simplicity. Georgie's brilliant personality, golden as her hair, had been the spontaneous, cheerful heart of their family. Josh—at first wary—had eventually thawed and even allowed David to adopt him legally. Mum—glamorous as always—had flitted in and out of their lives, loving and spoiling them all, while his work kept him busy and satisfied.

Perfection.

Which then began to fall, sickeningly, apart.

Georgie's death from an aneurism, just five short years into their marriage, had almost broken him, the pain and guilt too much to bear.

Josh—who'd needed him more than ever—and his work had been the only things keeping David going during the first year. Those commitments got him out of bed each day and forced him to put one foot in front of the other.

But fate wasn't done with him yet, as he found out all at once a year later.

A diagnosis of palmar fibromatosis put pay to his surgical career, just as he learned who his father had been and about the vast fortune he was to inherit. And when he realized his mother had been in contact with Sir Arthur over the years, David was incandescent with rage.

A rage that carried him through the legal battle and nasty rhetoric but left him cold and hollow inside, emotionally distant from everyone but Josh.

After all, with that much money in hand, who could he trust to be interested or invested in *him* rather than his fortune?

Once the courts had determined Sir Arthur's will was legitimate, David's mother had tried to calm the waters.

"Davie, if you just stay out of the spotlight, it will quiet down. You'll see."

He'd been too grief-stricken and angry—with her, with life—to listen. Instead, he'd taken a lump of his inheritance and created the Georgina Dolores Kennedy Foundation, dedicated to fostering transplant research, education, and networking. Then, as was his way, he committed himself to making the homage to his late wife work and grow, even as he maintained a consultancy practice as well.

Staying firmly in the spotlight allowed him to build the foundation into something truly worthwhile, and he was as committed to its growth as he'd ever been.

Putting his elbow on the door's armrest and leaning his chin on his fist, David stared out the window at the now driving rain and exhaled hard. It was a mark of his exhaustion that he was even thinking about the past this way. Normally, he tried to forget about those horrible, excruciating years and concentrate on the present and the future. And the immediate future was all about the upcoming rally.

Rally Round, originally envisioned as a short classic-car run in the vein of the London to Brighton race, had grown much larger. He'd thought it a good way to publicize the important work transplant teams were doing across the UK, but once his promotional team had begun consulting their contacts to gauge interest, it had ballooned.

And David had let it.

Not everyone was impressed with the widening scope, and a few foundation directors had voiced their concern regarding the amount of money now being spent. David pointing out that they'd already raised public awareness and spurred an important conversation centered around the need for organ and blood donations hadn't satisfied them.

"What you've done is wasted valuable time and resources and turned the foundation into a carnival, with you as the barker," Sir Malcolm, the most vocal of the opponents, had rudely stated.

It was no secret Malcolm's cadre would like nothing better than to oust David from his position as CEO and dismantle many of David's more progressive programs. To them, the foundation was on the verge of collapse because David was determined to take advantage of new technology, particularly social media, to increase visibility.

On top of everything else that was happening, having to deal with their nonsense was exhausting.

This trip to Liverpool had come up unexpectedly but was, in a way, a welcome distraction. As a part of his consultancy practice, he was often called in to evaluate high-risk potential transplant recipients. The young lady he was going to see had both type 1 diabetes and progressive kidney disease, and a decision had to be made as to whether it was suitable to put her on the transplant list.

Being out of his office at the foundation meant he was less accessible and could screen both calls and emails for urgency. He'd always maintained an open-door policy at the London headquarters, allowing people to drop in to his office for a chat or to update him, but he didn't have time for that just now.

For the next few days, his main focus would be on his patient, with the rally taking up whatever spare moments he had. But for these last few minutes, between the train station and the hospital, David tried to get his brain to slow and his shoulders to relax.

When his phone rang, he sighed.

Respite denied.

Then he smiled, as he saw Josh's name on the screen.

"Morning, Dad." Josh's voice made David's smile widen. "Heard you on the radio just now. You sounded like you were a hair's breadth from giving that reporter a frosty tongue-lashing."

David chuckled. "Well, *I* thought I was politely restrained."

Josh chuckled too. "You were, but barely. Did you make it to Liverpool all right?"

"I'm almost to the hospital."

"I'm close to work too but, I've been thinking…"

"Uh-oh. That sounds ominous."

Josh ignored his interruption. "Why don't you slow down a bit, after the rally?"

His son's words made his heart rate kick up and caused a cold ball to form in his chest. Making his tone amused and slightly distant was instinctual.

"Oh? Why? Do you think I'm getting decrepit?"

"No. I think you're overworked. You should get back to some of the things you love but don't do anymore."

There was a slight hesitation before he continued.

"It struck me when I heard you on the radio. I almost didn't recognize your voice. And when I was arranging the delivery of the Daimler, I thought about that Austin we'd been fixing up and never got going because you're always on the move. We should be driving that in the rally, not Mr. Granger's fancy auto."

Josh didn't need to elaborate. There were times when David found himself watching his own actions—hearing his own voice—as though from a distance and wondered who that man was. Yet, the change was effective and suited his purposes. After the way he and his character had been called into question, both in court and the press, a facade of distant arrogance had seemed the best way to react.

"Dad." Josh's voice brought him out of his thoughts, and he grunted in reply. "I know how important the foundation is to you, but you deserve a life of your own. A regular, happy life, instead of all this rushing about and stress."

"I *am* happy." Infusing enthusiasm into his voice was far harder than it should have been. "You know I get intense satisfaction from the work I'm doing."

"Yeah, I do, but think about what I've said anyway, okay?"

"I will." He wouldn't, but the lie tripped easily off his tongue. There was no reason to have Josh worrying unnecessarily.

"I'm just pulling into the hospital parking lot, so I have to go. Have a good day. Talk to you later."

"Love you, son."

And that was no lie. Adopting Josh and raising him after Georgie died were two things in his life David felt he'd done properly.

When he'd met Georgie, she'd been clear about not wanting any more children.

"I've made a hash of raising the one I already have," she'd said, with a glint in her eye that told him arguing wouldn't be a good idea. "If you want a child, you're best off looking elsewhere."

He'd already been too head over heels about her to care and, once they'd married, he'd happily taken on Josh as his own. No one knew that just before her death she'd changed her mind and they'd begun trying to get pregnant. Coming off the pill had thrown her reproductive system into disarray, but on the day she'd collapsed, she'd insisted David attend an all-day seminar, although admitting to a headache.

"Probably just hormones," she'd said, refusing his offer to stay home with her. "I'll take something and lie down for a little."

The guilt of his decision to do as she said would never leave him, no matter how many years went by. He'd failed to protect her, to be there when she needed him most, and still hadn't forgiven himself for that.

The rain eased slightly, and the traffic, which had slowed, picked up speed again. Pulling himself once more out of the past, he glanced at his watch. He should be on time for his appointment with the transplant-recipient coordinator, as the buildings of the St. Agnes Hospital were now visible, and the entrance was just around the next corner.

The car accelerated, and David opened his lips to tell the driver to slow down, but it was too late. With a whoosh, the vehicle hit a puddle, sending an arc of water toward the pedestrians hurrying along the sidewalk.

"Slower, please," he said sharply.

"Just trying to get you to your destination on time, sir."

"I'm sure the people walking to work would prefer I be a bit late so they don't get splashed with dirty water."

"Yes, sir."

Then, as the brief moments of inactivity were almost over, David prepared himself for his meeting and another long day.

Valerie Sterling squelched her way into the ladies' room down the corridor from her office, going as quickly as she could on her aching ankle. The lower part of her coat and legs were soaked, as were her shoes.

If the start of the day was any indication, it might have been better had she stayed in bed.

Yet, there was no time to whinge, which wasn't in her nature anyway. Dr. Kennedy was probably already in her office, and if she didn't hurry, she'd be late.

Between the rain, a bus that broke down long before her stop, and a near fall that had left her with a twisted ankle and a ball of fear in her stomach, she was frazzled.

Being liberally splashed by a passing car had been the final straw.

Getting herself presentable and calmed down before her meeting, all within seven minutes, wouldn't be easy. All she could hope was that Shala, the office assistant she shared with four other managers, wouldn't leave the consultant cooling his heels in the reception area. Sometimes the younger woman could be scatterbrained, and Val could see her doing just that.

Unable to stand comfortably on her right foot, she backed into a cubicle and sat on the closed toilet seat to remove her shoes one at a time and wipe her feet and legs. Thank goodness, once she'd seen the overcast sky, she'd packed her court pumps in her tote rather than wearing them.

Of course, if she'd accepted her neighbor's offer of a drive to work, none of this would have happened. But refusing Tony's offer had been instinctive, and Val had no regrets.

He'd just moved in and had already told anyone who'd listen that he was newly divorced. The few times they'd spoken, he'd gazed at Val with the sort of puppy-dog eyes that had probably initially got his ex to marry him but left Val unmoved.

One thing the long-ago breakup of her marriage had taught her was that being independent and single was smart and putting your happiness in someone else's hands was foolish.

The last thing she needed was to once more risk the type of embarrassment and heartbreak Des had caused.

With a grimace of pain, she got her right shoe on and stood up. The memory of falling, of the woman behind her grabbing her arm to stop her landing on the pavement, tried to intrude and had to be pushed aside.

She didn't know what had caused her to lose her balance, and that was terrifying. If she allowed herself to think about that now, her chances of concentrating in the upcoming meeting would be naught.

Yet the specter of multiple sclerosis was never far from her thoughts these days. And, as she limped out of the ladies' and toward her office, she couldn't help paying intense attention to the sensation of her muscles moving beneath her skin. Checking to make sure they were working the way they should.

Getting to the reception desk, she forced herself to smile at Shala while looking around for the consultant, who was nowhere in sight.

"I put him in your office, Mrs. Sterling," the

young woman whispered. "And called down to get you a pot of tea."

Leaning close, Val asked, "Has he been here long?"

Shala shook her head, causing her dangly earrings to dance. They were the kind of jewelry Val always admired but never bothered to buy, not thinking they'd suit her.

"No, he just got here."

Heaving a sigh of relief, Val straightened and replied, "Bring the tea in when it arrives, please."

"I will."

She'd got to her door when Shala said, "Are you okay, Mrs. Sterling?" Val paused and looked back, lifting her eyebrows. "You're limping."

"I'm fine," she replied, opening the door and stepping through before the younger woman could comment further.

"I'm sorry to keep you waiting," she said briskly, nudging the door shut and facing the man rising to his feet from the visitor's seat.

She'd planned to shrug off her coat, but the first sight of David Kennedy had her freezing in place for an instant, her heart doing a crazy flip-flop.

What a magnificent man.

"Not at all," he replied, his coolly polite words breaking her out of the trance she'd fallen under. "I only just got here myself."

Turning away, she pulled off her wet mackin-

tosh and hung it on the coatrack, her hands ridiculously clumsy and shaky. In her mind's eye,
she could still see him, and the image had tingles
running up and down her spine.

Oh, she'd seen him in the media and knew he
was handsome, but she'd been able to think so in
a distant, disinterested way. Up close, though, in
person, there was something downright electric
about the dark, intent gaze, the way he moved
with such fluid grace, and the rich, deep timbre
of his voice.

Dressed in a suit that fitted his broad shoulders
to perfection, his snowy-white shirt emphasiz-
ing the smooth, mocha-toned skin, Dr. Kennedy
was just a smidge shy of beautiful. His elegant
appearance, however, was perfectly balanced by
the strength of his facial features and the cool in-
telligence in his eyes.

She'd raised a hand to smooth her hair when
she realized what she was doing and let it fall.
Hadn't she read somewhere that a woman playing with her hair signaled sexual interest?

We'll have none of that, my girl.

Instead, she flattened her expression and, ignoring the warmth rising into her cheeks, made
herself walk across the room toward him, her
hand outstretched.

"It's a pleasure to meet you, Dr. Kennedy."

His fingers were warm, his handshake firm,

but Val had to stop herself from jerking away when her nerves jangled with delight at his touch.

"The pleasure is mine," he replied, and although his voice was still distant, his gaze seemed anything but, and Val had to turn away before she drowned in it.

Withdrawing her hand from his, she moved behind her desk to her filing cabinet, using the time it took to retrieve the patient's file to gather her shattered composure.

It was going to be a very long three days working with him if she couldn't get herself under control!

Taking a deep, silent inhale, she faced him and said, "Let's get on with it, shall we?"

CHAPTER TWO

DAVID TRIED TO keep his mind on what Valerie Sterling was saying but was constantly side-tracked by the cadence of her voice and the movement of her lips. When their gazes met, his breath caught in his chest, and he was forced to look away lest he get trapped staring into those beautiful aqua-shaded eyes.

Were they bluer or greener? They seemed to change, like the color of the ocean changes during a tempest.

Why did he even care?

But he did, and he tried to figure out why.

Valerie Sterling wasn't beautiful in conventional terms. Some people, noting her nondescript coloring and mousy hair, might even call her plain, yet there was an air about her that David found completely enthralling.

When she'd come in the door—damp blond wisps escaping her low ponytail, a bit of a flush on her cheeks—his heart had seemed to turn over, as though in joyful recognition. And although the handshake they'd exchanged was businesslike and just shy of perfunctory, his fingers still carried the phantom sensation of her skin beneath his.

Her turning away to unlock her filing cabinet left him immersed in a swirl of fresh, womanly scent that went straight to his head.

By the time her assistant pushed open the door and brought in a tea tray, David realized he'd said little to nothing but allowed her to carry the meeting. Even during the pause, while Mrs. Sterling poured, conversation lagged as he fought not to start peppering her with questions about herself.

Where was she from? Was she happily married? What caused her to limp? Did she find her work challenging and satisfying?

It was disquieting and should have had his stress rates through the roof. But strangely, his headache had subsided, even as he wondered at his distracted state and obsession with the no-nonsense woman across the desk.

"Tamika Watkiss's condition has undergone a sharp deterioration over the last month, as you can see from her records." She was completely professional, having already pointed out various test results she found pertinent, yet David was staring at the file in his hand like an imbecile, fighting to concentrate. "At this point, Dr. Laghari believes pancreas and kidney transplants may be her only hope for a normal life. However, there are factors other than her physical and mental condition I think may weigh heavily into the decision of whether to put her on the list or not."

"Oh?"

So stupid to feel almost tongue-tied in her presence, to have his usual eloquence drained away by the merest look in her direction. Self-consciousness made him sound even stuffier—stiffer—than usual, and he could hear her voice changing, becoming sharper with each sentence she spoke.

"Tamika's parents have very different ideas about what's best for her going forward, and those differences have to be taken into consideration. The family unit seems to be, up to this point, a strong one, but there is a distinct chance that if we're not careful, any course of treatment suggested may precipitate a family crisis."

"Which will also disrupt the patient's state of mind."

At least he had the wherewithal to make *one* sensible statement so far, but Valerie Sterling looked less than impressed.

"At the very least. Damage to her family could also potentially have far-reaching health effects for Tamika, whether she's suitable for surgery or not."

Why did it feel as though she were taking him to task? While he was impressed that she clearly didn't think his reputation merited special treatment, it still somehow stung. And when stung, he retreated further into his public persona.

Closing the file in his hand, he smiled the thin, barely there smile he used as a shield, and quietly said, "Well, it's early days to be worrying about that just yet. We still have all the testing to do, which is why I'm here. Have you set up a meeting with the patient and her parents?"

Valerie rocked back in her chair, and her eyes narrowed for an instant, but when she spoke it was in an even, colorless tone. "I informed them you'd be here today and would want to speak to them, yes."

Restless, wanting to be in motion and put some additional air and space between them, David rose and nodded toward the door.

"Shall we, then?"

"As you wish," she replied, getting to her feet and rounding the desk, the skin around her lips tight, her limp more pronounced. "Tamika's mother works nights and usually comes in first thing in the morning to sit with her for a few hours before going home to rest. She should be here by now."

He got to the door ahead of her and opened it, standing aside so she could precede him through, regretting the gentlemanly habit when it left him once more in the wake of her delicious scent.

Perhaps drawing it deep into his lungs wasn't the best option for his peace of mind, but that's what he did anyway.

What an ass!

If her ankle hadn't been so painful, Val would have marched down to the elevator in double time. As it was, all she could do was keep her back as straight as possible and her nose in the air while she limped along, fuming.

Apparently, Dr. David Kennedy had allowed his reputation to go to his head in a big way. He'd hardly spoken, dismissed her concerns regarding the situation between Mr. and Mrs. Watkiss, and, when she'd tried to explain her worries further, had called an abrupt end to the meeting.

If this was how he behaved with everyone, she'd have to be a buffer between him and the Watkiss family or be doing damage control continuously over the next few days.

The nerve of the man!

Oh, she knew he was highly qualified, and his foundation was doing an awful lot of good to educate both medical personnel and the public about the issues surrounding transplants, but come on! It didn't make him a deity. Not by a long shot.

She'd have a heck of a lot more respect for him if he'd continued to operate after inheriting that pile of money rather than all but abandoning his profession. If he had still been operating, she could put his attitude down to that famous surgeon arrogance so many medical practitioners had to put up with. As it was, he was just a consultant, and no matter how highly regarded he was, it was no excuse for bad manners.

She reached out to jab at the elevator button, but Dr. Kennedy beat her to it and their hands brushed, sending another of those tingling waves of sensation along her arm.

And damn him for affecting me this way.

Somewhere, in the midst of all the stress she'd been going through over the last little while, she must have lost her mind. That was the only explanation for this unwanted—and unwarranted—attraction.

Tense enough to crack, she worked on maintaining a frosty demeanor as they rode down in the elevator. She preceded him out of the lift and then down the corridor toward where Tamika's room was located. Making sure not to indicate which door she was going to until they were right at it, she pushed through without waiting for him to open it for her.

Tamika was sitting at a small table near the window, her laptop in front of her, some textbooks strewn around. When she looked up Val smiled, although she couldn't help noticing how poorly the teenager looked in comparison to when they'd first met. Her skin had lost both color and luster, giving it a grayish hue, and her wide brown eyes were sunken.

"Hi there," Val said, making her way into the room. Mrs. Watkiss was nowhere to be seen. "How're you doing today?"

Tamika scowled, her gaze going from Val to David and back again while she gestured to the books. "All right. But I'm trying to catch up with my schoolwork. I lost almost a whole year, and I really want to take my GCSEs next year, but they won't let me unless I'm up-to-date. Why're you limping?"

Val was suddenly under intense scrutiny not just from Tamika but from the man standing beside her too.

"Just a little mishap this morning, on my way to work. It's nothing. This is Dr. Kennedy," she added quickly before either of them could say a word. "He's the consultant I told you about a couple of days ago."

"Hi."

Tamika looked anything but excited to meet another doctor, but David went right over and held out his hand, giving her a warm smile.

"Hi," he replied, before pointing to her books. "What are you studying?"

"History," she answered, wrinkling her nose. "I hate it, so I kept putting it off."

David chuckled. "Was never one of my favorites either. I much preferred the sciences."

"I like math best, and I'm not too bad at English, but history…" She shook her head, smiling back at him. "All those dates and so many kings. It's ridiculous."

Pulling out the chair on the opposite side of the table, David sat down, still chuckling. "I agree. So much easier to remember the queens that ruled in their own names because there weren't as many."

"Yeah," she agreed, but with a little pout. "But I usually forget some of them too. If the answer isn't *Elizabeth* or *Victoria*, I probably don't know it."

David laughed outright then, the warm sound wrapping itself around Val in the most disquieting way. How on earth had that standoffish, arrogant ass morphed into this easy-going, comfortable man? A man able to win over an ill teenager, who was often out of sorts and cranky, with little to no effort?

He was asking her about her future plans as though it was a given that the desperately ill teen had a long life ahead of her. Val was surprised to hear the answer.

"Well, it's hard to make plans when you have brittle diabetes and chronic kidney disease, but what I'd really like to do is work out in the open, like on a farm, or a national park. If I can't do that, I think I'll write a book." The look she gave

David was level and unafraid. "A person has to have something constructive to do, right?"

Val turned away, so that Tamika wouldn't see the sheen of tears in her eyes. The young woman's courage in the face of life-threatening odds was both moving and inspiring.

"Yes." His voice was suddenly deeper, with a tone that seemed almost sad, although when Val glanced at him, he was still smiling. "Everyone needs a goal. I'll look forward to reading it."

"Your mum's not here yet?" Val asked, after a short silence that seemed too heavy to be allowed to continue for long.

"She went down to the caff to get some tea." Tamika looked down, and her fingers curled into little fists on her lap. "I keep telling her she should go home after work and get some rest, but she still comes every day anyway."

"No doubt because she couldn't rest until she'd seen you and made sure you were all right. I know that's what I'd do, if my son was in hospital and about to go through more testing."

Tamika looked up at him. "You have a son? How old is he?"

David smiled, and Val felt her heart do a crazy flip at the fondness in his expression.

"Josh is thirty-four, and before you say anything, I'd still be at the hospital every day if he was a patient."

Before she could reply, the door opened, and

Mrs. Watkiss came bustling in, pausing to say, "Oh, Mrs. Sterling, is this Dr. Kennedy? I hope I didn't keep you waiting."

Val touched her shoulder and smiled, shaking her head. "Not at all. We haven't been here long."

David had risen, and as they shook hands, Val's phone buzzed.

"Excuse me," she said, recognizing her assistant's number. "I have to take this. Will you be okay for now, Dr. Kennedy?"

"Of course." The look he sent her way made heat pool in her belly, although his voice was cool. "I'll find you when I'm finished here, if necessary."

And, still flustered, although there was no conceivable reason to be, she got out of there as quickly as she could, heaving a sigh of relief once the door had shut behind her.

Dr. David Kennedy was an arrogant, dismissive man, who apparently was exactly the type that attracted her.

How infuriating!

CHAPTER THREE

DAVID SPENT MOST of the rest of the morning with Mrs. Watkiss and Tamika, first just talking generally and then going over some of the tests Tamika would undergo starting the next day.

The Watkiss family, as it turned out, were originally from the Caribbean, although Tamika's parents were both born in England, where they'd met and married.

"My parents were from Grenada," Mrs. Watkiss told David. "And Ricardo's came here from Barbados."

They'd met at church when they were in their teens and had moved to Liverpool from London after Mr. Watkiss had gotten a job with what was then British Rail. He still worked with National Rail and was away from home on assignment periodically.

When David asked if he would be able to meet Tamika's father while he was in Liverpool, Mrs. Watkiss bit her lip and said she'd let her husband know he was wanted.

"He doesn't do so well in hospitals, you know," she said, and in his peripheral vision David noticed Tamika roll her eyes.

When he looked at the teen and raised an eyebrow, she shrugged and shook her head.

"Dad gets soppy whenever he comes to the hospital to see me," she said. "So I told him it was okay and I'd be home soon enough."

"Ricardo looks after Tamika if she's poorly, whenever he's home," Mrs. Watkiss supplied, as though standing up for her absent husband. "He's a good dad, isn't he, sweetie?"

"The best," Tamika said, throwing her mum a little smile. Then, as though very much wanting to get off the topic, she asked David, "Are your parents or grandparents from somewhere else, Dr. Kennedy? Or were they born here?"

Following her lead, David replied, "Actually, my mum was originally from the US."

Mrs. Watkiss's eyes widened, and she snapped her fingers, saying, "That's right! I was wondering where I knew your face from. Your mum is Cerise Kennedy, the singer, right?"

He should be used to it by now, but it took everything he had not to stiffen up and risk losing the rapport he'd been developing with Mrs. Watkiss.

"Yes," he said. "That's my mother."

"Who?" Tamika asked, her brow wrinkling.

David chuckled. "She was popular way before your time."

"Oh, you know who she is, Tam," Mrs. Watkiss said. "Your grandma Olive loved her songs. She'd play them all the time."

And then she started singing. "Some folks are green with envy, others sad and blue, but I'm just tickled pink, to be so loved by you."

Hearing his mother's trademark song brought a pang of sorrow, and although David kept smiling, a weight settled around his heart. It was as though, for an instant, he was transported back to childhood and Mum was leaning over him as he lay in bed, singing that song. To everyone else, "Love in Pink" was his mother's signature song, but to David it was, and always would be, *his* song.

"Oh, yes. I remember that." Tamika turned shining eyes toward David. "I love it. It reminds me of Gran."

"I know my mum would love to know that," he said softly.

"I haven't heard anything of her in a long time," Tamika's mother said. "Is she still with us?"

"Yes, she is," he replied. "Still performing too, but mostly on the Continent—France, Monaco, occasionally in Germany."

Then, before that curious gleam in the other woman's eyes could be given voice, he moved the conversation along to what Tamika and her mother could expect over the next few days.

"We'll be doing extensive testing, including a series of X-rays and ultrasounds, to make sure Tamika is healthy enough to potentially undergo surgery."

As he went over the various tests, outlining what each one was, Mrs. Watkiss listened intently, but he could see Tamika's attention wandering. Eventually, she sighed.

"Mrs. Sterling went over all of this with Mum and me already," she said.

David nodded, ignoring the way his pulse jumped at the mention of Valerie Sterling. "I'm sure she did. But it's my job, ultimately, to make the decision as to whether you'll be placed on the transplant list or not, so I have to be very careful that you and your parents understand exactly what's happening at any given time."

"Hush, Tamika, and let Dr. Kennedy talk."

But as her mother scolded her, David could see a stubborn twist to the young woman's lips, and he smiled, saying, "I'm finished for now, Mrs. Watkiss, and I know you probably need to get home to get some rest. I'll be in tomorrow morning, so I'll see you then."

Tamika nodded, not meeting his eyes as she mumbled goodbye, and her mother rose to walk with David to the door, then out into the corridor. Putting her hand on his arm, she looked up at him with an expression of almost overwhelming gratitude.

"Thank you, Dr. Kennedy. I know my daughter is in the best of hands and you'll do everything you can to make her well."

It was at times like this that David, for all his experience, felt a visceral sense of inadequacy. All he could do was pat Mrs. Watkiss's hand and say, "I'll try to make the best decisions for Tamika's care, Mrs. Watkiss. Please ask your husband to let me know when he's available so I can make sure to keep my schedule open."

That seemingly distracted her from whatever else she was planning to say and, when he opened the door for her, she went back into her daughter's room.

Standing in the corridor for a moment, he considered all he'd learned that morning about his patient and her mother. While, as a part of her assessment, there would be a psychologist examining Tamika and speaking to both her parents, David believed there was much to be learned by simply meeting them himself. That was the real reason he'd come to Liverpool. The doctors at St. Agnes Hospital were perfectly capable of running all the tests needed, and he could have stayed in London and had all the results sent to him for his evaluation.

That had never been—and would never be—

the way he worked. He might no longer be capable of operating on patients himself, but both patients and their surgeons deserved every ounce of skill he could muster so as to achieve the best possible outcomes. And that meant being engaged and involved from the start of the assessment process all the way through to whatever the end might be.

Valerie Sterling might not be impressed by him, but he wasn't there for her approbation, so her questioning, sharp manner shouldn't matter.

Yet it did.

And why on earth was he even thinking about her instead of concentrating on his patient, or even Rally Round? No doubt there were a hundred emails and phone messages waiting for his attention, not to mention his meeting with the team of doctors taking care of Tamika.

All of those matters were a lot more important than the icy woman with changeable, sea-storm eyes, who clearly had no use for him.

A woman who, he'd learned from Tamika's reaction, didn't normally have a limp but had hurt herself on the way to work. The stubborn woman hadn't even stopped to get it looked after before their meeting.

Shaking his head, David strode toward the nurses' station, a crazy, absolutely ill-advised plan forming in his head.

* * *

Val looked up as a knock sounded on her door and grinned as her friend, hepatologist Emma Owen, stuck her head into the office.

"Are you busy?"

"Come in," Val replied, closing the file she'd been going over and pushing it to one side. Glancing at her watch she realized how late it was getting. "Heading down to lunch?"

"Already had mine," Emma replied, flopping into the visitor's chair and twitching a stray piece of her red hair behind her ear. "But I have a few minutes before my next meeting and wanted to firm up our plans for the rally."

"What's to firm up?" Val shifted her legs and tried not to wince when her ankle throbbed in protest. "We've got rooms booked through the foundation and time off arranged."

"Yes, but…" Val's antennae vibrated as her younger friend grinned. "What about costumes?"

Val sat up straighter in her chair. "Costumes? What costumes?"

"Well, I was putting together a soundtrack for the rally—sixties music, to go with the Mini— and thought, wouldn't it be cool for us to have some sixties clothes to carry on the theme?"

"No. No, no, no." Val kept talking over Emma's peel of laughter. "Sixties fashions were all miniskirts and go-go boots, weren't they? That's so not my idea of fun."

"Oh, come on, Val. Live a little. I've found a bunch of stuff in thrift stores and online, so you're coming over to my place this evening to try some on. I won't take no for an answer."

Live a little.

As Val looked at her friend, the words echoed in her mind.

She'd been so bogged down with responsibilities over the past years she'd fallen into a seemingly never-ending whirl of motion, none of it fun, a lot of it frightening or saddening. Watching her mother deteriorate, working all hours possible to keep the family's heads above water, then losing Mum, and having both Clayton and Liam move out...

She'd felt wrung out, used up, and rather bitter that her youngest son had decided to go and live with his father—the same man who'd abandoned them years before.

But, most of all, fear of the future had stalked her mind continuously.

Multiple sclerosis was now assumed to be genetic—or at least have a genetic component. Not only had Mum suffered from it, but Val was pretty sure her grandmother had too, although forty-plus years ago the doctors hadn't diagnosed it as such. More and more often, in moments of quietude, Val found her brain circling back to MS, chewing over what she would do should she discover she had it.

At those times, the thought of being a burden, of having one of her children have to take care of her, or going to a nursing home sat like a rock in her stomach.

She couldn't figure out which was worse.

Her GP had told her, "There's no need to worry about it. Just watch for symptoms, and come back to see me if you experience any."

That was, in her opinion, absolutely no help whatsoever.

The symptoms were legion and ranged across the board from physical pain to mental fog, with a host of others in between.

How was she to know whether a sudden fall was due to slippery pavement or MS? Whether her inability to concentrate was due to a long hard day or MS?

Realizing fear of the disease was wearing her down as quickly as the disease itself would, she knew she had to make peace with it somehow. And when Emma had asked her to run the GDK Foundation rally with her and act as navigator, it had sparked something inside. A sense of adventure she'd completely forgotten existed in her soul. Maybe MS was her future, but wasn't that the very best reason to live fully now?

"Oh, all right," she said, earning a fist pump from Emma. "I'm free this evening."

"Brilliant. Text me when you're finished here,

and we can leave together. My larder is bare, so we'll pick up something to eat on the way."

Before Val could reply, there was another knock on her door. Emma got up, as Val called out for the person to come in.

When David Kennedy stepped into her office, Val's heart started to race, and it took everything she had inside to keep her expression coolly questioning.

"David, how lovely to see you." Having Emma greet him like a long-lost friend took Val aback. She knew they'd probably have come in contact before, through work, but this seemed a lot more personal. "I thought you'd be in London, getting the rally sorted."

"Emma, good to see you too." The fondness in his expression was unmistakable and left Val wondering if he'd reserved his stiff arrogance just for her. "I got called in for a consult, and I'm sure the foundation staff have all the rally details under control."

Emma chuckled, as they hugged briefly. "As though that would stop you from poking your nose into everything anyway."

David shook his head and gave her a narrow-eyed look, his arm still slung companionly over her shoulders. "Are you saying I'm incapable of delegating?"

"Would I be so rude?" she deadpanned in return.

"Touché, young lady." He gave her shoulders one last squeeze and then let her go, asking, "So how are you? And how's that liver donor faring?"

Emma was on a team supervising a live liver donor, in preparation for the proposed transplant, now about six weeks away.

"Everything is going well with the donor, and I'm getting ready for Rally Round. Val and I are running it together, in Dad's Mini."

David's gaze swung to Val's face for a moment and left her breathless, with sparks firing along her nerve endings from just that fleeting glance.

"Have you run a rally before?" he asked, his attention back on Emma, leaving Val able to collect herself, although she found it more difficult to do than she liked.

"I haven't, but Val has." Emma was quite happy to supply the information, unaware of the strange tension in the room. "She used to navigate for her brother when she was younger."

"Did she, now?" There was something about his voice—slightly mocking, as deep and dark as midnight-blue velvet—that caused a shocking reaction deep in her belly. Val looked down at her desk, hopefully masking her expression. "Mrs. Sterling is a lady of many talents."

"She's wonderful," Emma replied. "She looked after Dad during the last year of his life and treated him as though he were family. Oops, I have to run," she added suddenly and much to

Val's relief. "I have a patient in a few minutes. Good to see you, David, and I'll see you later, Val."

Then she was gone, and Val suddenly wasn't as happy about her leaving as she'd been a few moments before. Although Emma wasn't there to spill anything more about Val's life, with her gone Val was suddenly alone with the handsome, disquieting man whose focus was now squarely on her.

Swallowing was more difficult than it should be. Meeting his gaze was even harder.

Taking a deep breath in through her nose, Val gathered her control and lifted her eyebrows.

"Is there something I can help you with, Dr. Kennedy?"

"Actually," he said, the cool, lazy tone once more in his voice, "I came to see if you'd had your ankle looked after."

Completely taken by surprise, Val stammered, "If-if what...?"

"Let me see it."

By his tone you'd think he was asking for a chart or an X-ray rather than one of her extremities. By the way her heart kicked into high gear, you'd have thought he was asking to see something far more personal than her ankle.

Hoping he'd put the rush of color heating her cheeks down to temper rather than anything else, she said, "My ankle is fine, Dr. Kennedy. There's no need to fuss."

"Did you bandage it?"

She'd meant to but, concentrating on work, had forgotten. Then, once she'd sat at her desk, hadn't wanted to get back up and find a bandage.

Not that she'd tell him any of that!

He came around to her side of the desk and went down on one knee. Cupping his hand, he repeated, "Let me see."

The terse way he spoke, the demand in his voice, should have put her back up, but somehow the sight of him kneeling at her feet, those long, dark fingers beckoning, undid her.

He was looking up at her, his eyes dark and unfathomable, his lips firm and somewhat stern, yet eminently kissable. Then he looked down to where her legs were curled to one side beneath her desk, and she realized he had the most ridiculously lush, black lashes.

It was as though time slowed and her brain—usually so unyielding and resolute—went into a state of quiescence unlike any she'd known. Without conscious thought, she swung her chair to the side and, extending her leg, placed the sore ankle into his waiting palm.

"It's swollen," he said, his fingers gently palpating the joint. "But not too bad. I'd suggest rest and elevating it for a while, but something tells me I'd be wasting my breath."

To her shock, he eased off her shoe before placing her foot on his thigh. Val's toes curled at the sensation of hard muscle beneath her plantar fascia, and when he twisted to reach into his jacket, she suppressed a gasp as those muscles shifted.

He brought out a bandage from his pocket and, before she could recover her senses enough to object, began to expertly wrap her ankle.

"I hope you have someone at home to help you so you can stay off your feet tonight."

He was still looking down at what he was doing, and Val was transfixed by the sight of his hands as he worked.

"I live alone," she replied, hearing her own voice as though from afar, experiencing this moment—so simple, really—as though they were involved in a deep intimacy.

Heart racing, toes still curled, heat pooling deep inside, her body reacting in a way she'd begun to think it never would again.

David secured the bandage but kept her foot in his hand, his thumb stroking, just once, along the skin at the base of her calf, causing a hard shiver of reaction along her spine. When he looked up at her, she wondered if any of what she was feeling was written on her face.

God, she hoped not!

"Well, stay off it as best you can."

"I will."

His eyebrows rose. "Will you? I know medical personnel make the worst patients so I have my doubts."

Their words were completely normal. Prosaic. Ordinary. Yet Val couldn't avoid the sensation of falling—into his voice, his gaze.

Wanting to slip off her chair and into his arms.

When he set her foot gently down on the carpet, the sense of loss was unmistakable.

As gracefully as he'd knelt, he rose.

"I'm off to meet Tamika's team and then to lunch with your CEO," he said, pushing back his cuff to glance at his watch. "But if you need me for anything—anything at all—contact me immediately."

And then suddenly, while she sat there undone and breathless, he was gone, leaving her staring at the door, trying to recover.

Hoping contact with him over the next couple of days would be minimal or preferably nonexistent.

CHAPTER FOUR

VAL'S HOPE TO not see David Kennedy again during his time at St. Agnes was scotched a couple of hours later when she got a message saying that Tamika Watkiss wanted to speak to him.

"I'll see if I can contact Dr. Kennedy," she told the nurse.

"I'm sorry, Mrs. Sterling," she was told. "I wasn't clear. Tamika is asking to speak to you both, preferably today."

When she checked, David was still in the hospital, finishing up lunch in the executive dining room. Sighing to herself, still annoyed at her earlier reaction to him, Val asked the CEO's personal assistant to give him the message.

A short time later the PA called back to say Dr. Kennedy would meet Val at Tamika's room in fifteen minutes.

Eschewing her pumps, which wouldn't fit properly with the bandage on her ankle anyway, Val put her still-damp flats back on and made her way down to the third floor. When she got off the elevator and saw David standing there, her silly heart did another of those flips, but by now she'd had time to gather her composure and greeted him with a nod.

"Do you know what's going on?" he asked, as they headed toward the young woman's room.

"I don't," she replied, trying to match his laconic tone. "The nurse didn't say."

Tamika was in bed, sitting up watching TV, and she didn't smile when they came in.

"I don't want to go on the transplant list," she said flatly, her chin jutting in a way that heralded her combative stance. Her gaze went from David to Val and then back again, as though daring them to argue. "So don't bother wasting time and money on all those tests you want to do."

"Okay," David said, pulling the two visitor's chairs closer to the bed, and waiting for Val to sit down before he did. "Would you mind telling me why?"

"What does that matter?" she said, her voice wobbling just a bit at the end. "I don't want it, and you can't make me."

"Of course we can't make you, and we wouldn't dream of forcing you to do anything you don't want to." His tone was easy, gentle, and yet not the tone of an adult speaking to a child but of one adult to another. "But knowing what you're thinking and why you feel this way might help our team understand other patients better."

Val could see the young woman absorbing his words, and her belligerent air seemed to dissipate somewhat.

"I…" She hesitated, as tears glimmered in her ears. "I don't want someone to have to die to help me."

David nodded slowly. "Understandable. But I can't help wondering if you truly know what you're saying."

"What do you mean?" Tamika went once more right into fight mode, making Val want to interject, but before she could. Tamika continued. "Of course I understand. It's been explained over and over, and I looked it up on the internet too. Some people can get transplants from live donors, but I can't. Someone would have to die before I could get a pancreas."

"Very true," David agreed. "But the reality is putting you on the transplant list doesn't mean someone is going to die to give you a pancreas. In fact, if you're not on the list and a donor that could be a match to you dies, chances are their pancreas and kidneys may go to waste, making a good thing they tried to do not happen."

Tamika's brow creased. "What do you mean?"

"I mean, people who go on the donor lists do it because they're trying to help others. They're being altruistic and hope that even when they die, they can still do some good in the world. Finding matches for our patients is often very hard to do, and since you looked it up online, you must know that just being on the list—if you are placed on it at all—doesn't mean we'll find you a match."

"I know. But if you did…"

She looked down, her hands fisted, a solitary tear trickling down her cheek. David reached over and pulled a tissue out of the box on the bedside table.

"If we did," he said gently, holding the tissue out to Tamika, "it means that someone has died and that there's nothing more we can do for them. But it also means that we're fulfilling a wish they had—that they wanted to give someone else a chance of a better life. Leave a legacy of hope behind. It's a wonderful, noble thing to do, I think. Don't you?"

Tamika took the tissue and scrubbed at her face, not answering for a moment. Then she looked up.

"Are you on the donor list?"

David smiled. "Of course."

"I am too," Val added. "My cousin's little boy needed a bone-marrow transplant years ago, and when I got tested, I signed up for life."

"Did he get one?"

Val wanted to lie but knew it wouldn't help.

"No, he didn't. Back then the match had to be even better than it can be now, and they couldn't find one close enough."

Tamika bit her lip, considering that, her gaze tracking back and forth between them.

"It's not that I don't appreciate what you're trying to do for me, it's just that I'm not sure I want to go through with a transplant, even if that means…"

Val knew what she'd been about to say, and David did too. What do you say to a sixteen-year-old who was staring her own mortality in the face?

A wave of anger spiked through Val's body, as often was the case in situations like this, but she tempered it so as to say, "It's a big decision, Tamika, and not one you have to make alone. Have you talked to your parents about this?"

Tamika shook her head. "I won't know what to say. Mum is always so cheery, as though everything is really okay, and Dad just looks so sad and tired. He works all the time, probably so he doesn't have to think about it all. I know eventually I need to bring it up with them, but I really don't know how."

"It is difficult, but really it's best if you at least share your fears and worries with them so they can help you. But, in the meantime, may I suggest at least going ahead with the testing, so you can keep your options open?"

"You don't have to make a decision today," David added. "Just think about it, okay? Remember, we still have a way to go before we know whether you'll be a good candidate to even get on the list, so there's no rush to decide."

"All right." Tamika nodded slowly. "I'll think about it, like you said."

"Good. Anything else you'd like to talk about or to know?"

Tamika shook her head. "No. But thank you for coming to talk to me. A lot of the doctors won't talk to me or explain things. They only talk to Mum."

"That's a shame, but in many cases they're aware that you're not old enough to sign on for surgeries or treatments, so they concentrate on your mother because she can give consent. The fact is, though, that you're the one who has to live with the consequences of whatever decisions are made."

"Exactly." Tamika looked fierce for a moment and then shook her head. "Explain that to Mum, though."

"I know how she feels," Val said, a pang of sadness squeezing her heart. "I don't care how old my boys get, they're still my babies. They're nineteen and sixteen and tell me off for treating them like they're still six sometimes, but I don't listen."

That made Tamika smile, just a little, and she said, "Okay, I get it. I don't have to like it, though, do I?"

Neither of the adults were going to encourage

rebellion so they just chuckled, and a few minutes later they said their goodbyes and left her room.

Just as they got outside the door David turned to her, and the expression on his face made her heart ache.

"*That's* why I set up the foundation," he said, the passion in his voice, in his eyes, unmistakable. "So that people like Tamika have a chance for a better life. It will only happen right now if we can improve the donor system—make it more diverse and increase the numbers of people who sign up."

He took a couple of steps away and then strode back to snare her gaze with his and hold it, effortlessly, as he spoke again.

"Hopefully one day we won't need transplants, whether of pancreas or islets. Researchers are so close to developing an artificial pancreas, but in the meantime all we're left with is donor transplantation, which too many people eschew. And that's why Rally Round and all educational initiatives surrounding transplant and blood donations are so important."

It was as though she were seeing him, the real Dr. David Kennedy, for the first time. Gone was the air of arrogance, the lazy superiority. Even the easy way he'd spoken to Tamika and Emma had only given a hint of who he really was. Now Val could see the man behind the mask, and he was one of substance and conviction, who she found even more attractive.

And far too magnetic.

She pulled herself together and started walking down the hallway toward the elevator, needing to be in motion and not simply stand there, enraptured, staring at him like a besotted idiot.

Clearing her throat, she replied, "You're preaching to the choir. I'll never understand people's reluctance to signing up to be a donor. It seems such a simple, yet important, thing to me."

"Exactly," he replied, keeping pace with her and then, when they got there, reaching out to push the button for the elevator. "But then, people don't make wills either, even when they have families depending on them to put their lives in good order."

"As though by just thinking about death, they're calling it to them." She shook her head, hoping he was looking at her, but unwilling to make eye contact. The potency of her attraction to him had been rising all day but now threatened to overwhelm her. "And by ignoring it, they can somehow stave it off."

"I suppose we're exposed to death more than most," he replied, as they entered the elevator. "So we're resigned to the fact that it comes for us all, eventually, and often when it's least expected."

She knew his story, or at least what had been

written about in the newspapers and gossip columns over the years. His wife had died years before, suddenly and while still young, so he obviously knew what he was talking about. Yet, although there was no bitterness or overt grief in his voice, she had to resist the urge to touch his hand in sympathy.

"*Resigned*?" she countered, making her tone sharply questioning to disguise her softer emotions. "I'm not sure about that. We might be accepting, even recognize the inevitability of it, but we still hold out hope right to the end. At least, that's been my experience." Then, because it felt as though their conversation were getting way too personal, she added, "How did you come up with the rally idea anyway?"

They were back on the floor where her office was, and he matched his far-longer strides to her shorter, limping ones.

"I've always liked cars," he replied. "When I was young, my mother's chauffeur let me hang about and tinker, and he taught me a lot about engines. As soon as I left home, I bought an old banger and fixed it up and continued to do that over the next few years."

He paused, as if the conversation had taken his attention somewhere else for a second, before he continued. "So when I was trying to come up with an idea to attract attention to the work transplant teams were doing, the two things just came together in my mind, and Rally Round was born."

"Are you driving a car of your own, that you fixed up?"

She risked a glance his way, so aware of him that her side tingled at his proximity and saw his lips turn down.

"Unfortunately, the vehicle I had started repairing with Josh isn't finished, so I've had to borrow a classic car for the rally."

"Oh, what kind?"

"I have an Austin Healey, but there's way too much left to be done on it to run a rally. Makes me wish I'd kept my old Anglia."

She could picture him in a sporty Austin, but the thought of him in an Anglia amused her no end.

"And what will you be driving in the rally?"

It seemed he hesitated for an instant before replying, "A 1930s Daimler, loaned to me by a friend."

That made her snort.

"Fancy, and somehow appropriate, since you're the master of ceremonies for the entire rally."

It was strange, but she immediately felt him withdraw, although she wasn't sure how she knew. Then, when he spoke, she knew her feeling was correct.

"Or, perhaps, the barker at the carnival."

The cool distance was back, and somehow she wasn't able to stomach it the way she had before.

So she stopped where she was to look up at him, eyebrows raised. "A barker, at the carnival? Really, Dr. Kennedy, I can't decide whether you're being snide or sniffing for compliments, so I won't even comment."

Then, even with her bandaged ankle, she set as brisk a pace as she could toward her office.

He caught up to her just outside her door and put his hand on the knob, as though to say something, but thankfully Shala interrupted.

"Mrs. Sterling, Mr. Watkiss just called and is asking to see you. He wonders if five this afternoon will be all right as he can stop by after work."

"I can meet with him then, if that suits," David replied before Val could.

Shala hesitated and then said, "He didn't ask for you, Dr. Kennedy. Only Mrs. Sterling."

"Really? I'd asked his wife to tell him I wanted to see him. I assumed he would be coming so we could meet."

"Call and tell him that will be fine, thank you, Shala. Don't mention anything about Dr. Kennedy, though."

"Yes, Mrs. Sterling."

As she went through the door into her office, Val said, "I'm not surprised he's trying to avoid you. He probably just wants me to tell you what he said. It's a wonder he's actually even coming in rather than just speaking to me on the phone."

It was then she realized he was standing just inside the door, making no attempt to come in any farther.

He shrugged, glancing down at his watch and saying in that annoyingly laconic way he had, "Too bad. I'll be back at five, and Mr. Watkiss can tell me himself what he thinks I should know. In the meantime, I have some work to do."

Then, while she stood there like a ninny, watching, he stepped back out of the office and was gone.

CHAPTER FIVE

DAVID STARED AT his computer screen, realizing he'd read the same sentence three times and still had no idea what it said. Since being set up in an unused office on the executive floor and opening his laptop, his concentration had been severely lacking.

It wasn't as though he didn't have gobs of work to do. At that very moment, he had at least ten documents open on his screen and another dozen or so internet tabs. And that didn't include the thirty or so emails he'd flagged for replies.

This really was the worst possible time to have his attention diverted to a woman.

Even if that woman was enthralling and compelling.

Sighing, David rose and walked over to the window, looking out over the rooftops below, trying to regain some sort of perspective.

Yes, Val Sterling did crazy things to his equilibrium. There was no way to deny that. But what was also undeniable was the fact he had no time for any type of relationship. Not even for a casual fling, should she be interested in one.

Between the foundation and his consultancy work, the rounds of galas and fundraising events, his life and schedule were constantly full. Now, with Rally Round coming up, he hardly had time to breathe. It took everything he had to keep it all straight and moving forward properly.

The best thing to do would be to stop thinking about Valerie Sterling as an attractive woman and think of her only in her official capacity.

Even as the thought entered his mind, his fingers flexed, as he recalled the softness of her skin and the fragrance that teased him whenever they were close together. There was nothing about her he found off-putting—and far too much about her he found enticing. Which, in itself, was strange and disquieting.

It wasn't as though he'd been a monk since Georgie died, but none of the women he'd dated casually had had this effect. Most had been attractive, some were even heralded as beautiful by the press, who seemed overly interested in reporting who he was seen with, but not one of them had disrupted his focus. He'd easily been able to concentrate on work, keeping the state of his private life completely separate and on the back burner.

Surely he could do the same with Val Sterling? Yet, just thinking about her had his pulse pounding and his body reacting in a most unsuitable way. There was something about her—an undefinable, yet completely overwhelming aura—that wouldn't allow him to simply block her out.

Instead, he wanted to know more about her. Her likes and dislikes, how her mind worked, and what it sounded like when she laughed. Whether she was always so sharp-tongued or if she had a softer side with not just her patients but others too.

He could, he thought, drown in her eyes and not care at all that his breath was being stolen. There was a need to explore her lips, learn their shape and texture and taste with his tongue, until he knew them as intimately as humanly possible.

And it wasn't just her lips he wanted to explore. Her softly rounded body, decorously dressed in a tailored, businesslike suit, made him want to unwrap it, until it lay bare before him and he could touch and savor every inch.

As he'd knelt at her feet bandaging her ankle, he'd wished he had the right to gently stroke his palm up along her leg, discovering the smooth skin of her calf then thigh. He'd actually imagined caressing her, until her legs parted in invitation and his hand could go higher...

Stop that, he said to himself, uncomfortable—both emotionally and physically—and a little appalled at his own turn of thought. *She's a co-*

worker, and thinking like that is completely inappropriate. You'd fire anyone you heard saying something like that.

Annoyed now, and determined to get as much work done as he could before their five-o'clock meeting, he went back to the desk and randomly pulled up one of the emails needing a reply. Forcing himself to concentrate, he noted it was from the production company that would be filming and putting together a documentary about the rally. They wondered, were there any of the participants he could recommend as interesting interview subjects during the two-week race?

Both Josh and he had agreed to take part, but there were aspects to transplantation that could best be illuminated by medical professionals other than surgeons.

Involving Valerie Sterling would give him a chance to get to know more about her, without displaying his interest. Picking up his phone, he called Emma Owen.

She picked up after just a couple of rings.

"Hi, David. What can I do for you?"

"I've had a request from the production company for suggestions of people they can interview during the rally to get a wide perspective on why people are participating. They're also interested in talking to folks intimately involved in the transplantation process, so I thought of you—and Mrs. Sterling."

"Oh, I'd definitely be willing, and I'm sure Val would be too. Do you want me to tell her about it?"

"If you don't mind," he replied. While he certainly could approach Val with the idea himself, he was sure she'd be more willing to agree if Emma did the asking. "Just let me know when you have a definitive answer."

"I should have one by this evening."

After he rang off, David glanced at his watch. Still another couple of hours to go before his meeting with Mr. Watkiss. Instead of being glad he had additional time to work, he found himself annoyed that the afternoon was going so slowly, and he had to give himself a mental shake.

"Enough." He said it aloud, for emphasis. "Concentrate."

But it took every scintilla of control he could muster to do so, and he couldn't help glancing at his watch periodically.

By four forty-five, his computer was packed and he was on his way down to Val's office, far too eager to get there and see her again.

He'd hardly had a chance to greet her before her assistant announced Tamika's father's arrival.

Ricardo Watkiss was a large, broad-shouldered man, as tall as David and with a crushing handshake. But for all his apparent strength, his gaze was that of an old man, leaving David with an impression of frailty and fear.

"I didn't want to bother you, Dr. Kennedy," he said, after they'd all sat down. "Mrs. Sterling knows how I feel about all of this and could have just told you."

"I'd rather hear it from you," David replied. Yet, it was already clear why Tamika's father hadn't wanted to speak to another doctor about his daughter. Already his eyes were damp, and he knotted his fingers together, as though seeking an anchor in an ever-shifting world. "Just take your time and tell me what you're thinking."

Ricardo took a breath, but it shuddered into his lungs, as though he found it hard to inhale.

"From what all the doctors have told me, my Tamika is dying." He paused and swallowed before continuing. "And what I want—what I think is best for her—is for her to come home so I can take care of her, keep her safe and comfortable, for as long as possible."

His anguish was obvious, his pain undeniable, and David's heart went out to him, even as he considered how best to approach the discussion.

"Mr. Watkiss, Tamika *is* gravely ill, and I know the odds of finding her a donor are slim, but don't you think it's worth exploring that option?"

Ricardo Watkiss shook his head. "Having her poked and prodded more? Do you know what she's gone through since the time she was six years old? Needles every day. Sticking her fingers, injecting herself. In and out of hospital, her blood sugar uncontrollable. We almost lost her a few times."

"But if she finds a donor, her life will be extended."

"But everyone says she probably *won't* find a donor." He held up his hands, fingers fisted, as though prepared to fight. "Why put her through all the tests, the pain, only for it to be false hope?"

Once more a member of the Watkiss family reminded David of his impotence when it came to the most important things in life, and for a moment he was at a loss as to how to proceed. Then Val Sterling spoke.

"Mr. Watkiss, we're all parents here, and I think I can speak for Dr. Kennedy when I say I don't know what you're going through. But what I do know is that you love your daughter and want only the best for her, am I right?"

"Exactly," he said, with an emphatic nod. "And that's not being subjected to a bunch of tests that won't do her any good."

"But none of us know whether they will do her good or not. Whether she's a fit candidate for the transplant list or not. Why wouldn't you at least want to know that? If she's not a good candidate, well, then you take her home, the way you want to. If she is a good candidate and goes on the list, then…"

"Then we're sitting there, waiting for something that won't happen, living in a fool's paradise."

His passionate interjection roused something deep inside David, and he had to reenter the discussion.

"No, Mr. Watkiss. If Tamika goes on the transplant list, there is hope, and it isn't false as you describe it. Hope never is false as long as it's true. And no matter what the future holds, Tamika needs to know you're as hopeful for her as her mother is. Otherwise, don't you think she'll believe you've given up on her?"

"Tam would never think that. She knows I love her more than anything. But I can't bear to think of her waiting, getting sicker, and being disappointed in the end. Her mother..." His voice cracked, and he had to clear his throat. "Bless her, but Lena is so sure Tamika will get well, I don't know what will happen to her if we have this hope for a miracle hanging over our heads and it doesn't come true."

"What will happen to her if you take away that hope?"

Val's quiet words seemed to shock Ricardo Watkiss. His eyes went wide, and his mouth moved, as though he were repeating what she'd said. When she continued to speak, his gaze never wavered but stayed glued to Val's face.

"Mr. Watkiss, what Tamika needs right now are her parents united. She has to know that, no matter what, you and your wife will be right there with her, and right there with each other. One of the things I worry about most is your family unit staying together and staying strong. No matter how this pans out, whether Tamika gets on the transplant list or not, whether she receives the transplant she needs or not, she needs you—both of you—by her side.

"What she doesn't need is to see her parents' marriage fall apart because you can't agree on her care. She doesn't need to see her siblings suffer more than they already are because of her illness."

"But—"

Val held up her hand, stopping him mid-interruption.

"Mr. Watkiss, I know from speaking to both of you that your and your wife's hopes and expectations about Tamika's health are very different. But there has to be a middle ground, and it is up to you, as Tamika's father, as the one who is determined to look at this situation from every angle, to find it."

"Mrs. Sterling is right." David leaned forward and met the other man's gaze. "I don't agree with your pessimism, but I certainly understand why you feel that way. Seeing your beloved daughter go through all she has must have torn you up inside, but now is not the time to give up or to lose courage. No matter what happens, your daughter needs you, and she always will."

Ricardo Watkiss dropped his chin to his chest and covered his eyes with his hand. His shoulders shook slightly and sounds of his rasping breaths filled the room. When he finally lifted his head, his eyes were red-rimmed, and his lashes were still wet.

"What should I do?" The agonized cry tore at David's heart, and in his peripheral vision he saw Val Sterling shift in her seat. "All I want is what's best for our family—for Tam—and I don't know what that is."

"Mr. Watkiss." David kept his voice quiet and waited until the other man looked at him before he continued. "Neither Mrs. Sterling nor I can tell you what the best course of action is, but my suggestion would be to talk with Tamika and—most importantly—with your wife. Just remember that your wife needs to cling to her hope that Tamika's life might improve, and Tamika, although she can't make the decision herself, needs to be listened to and her wishes taken into account."

Ricardo nodded slowly and took a deep breath.

"I'm frightened for Tamika, and for Lena too."

"It's good that you can admit it," Val said gently. "Some men just shut themselves off from situations like this, and that can only make things worse. Like Dr. Kennedy said, speak to your wife and Tamika, and, just as importantly, *listen* to what they have to say. This decision is one best made among the family and out of love and caring, not fear and hopelessness."

There was a change in the man's demeanor, as though those words had given him renewed strength, helping him sit up a bit straighter, leaching some of the worry from his face.

"I'll do that," he said. "And I guess there can't be too much harm in Tamika getting those tests. At least that way, if you say she's a good candidate and she decides she wants to be on the list, we'll have that information to hand."

David nodded, hiding his relief behind a neutral expression. It wasn't that he was invested in getting Tamika Watkiss on the transplant waiting list. Indeed, as he kept telling her parents, there was much to be done to even determine whether she was eligible to go on it or not. But the bottom line was, in his opinion, her best chance of extending her life expectancy was a transplant, and if she could get on the list she'd have a chance, no matter how slim, of getting one.

Ricardo Watkiss was taking his leave, and David stood up to shake his hand. Then he watched Val Sterling walk him to the door, while his brain shifted gears, focusing once more on the transplant-recipient coordinator.

Val shut the door and limped back to her chair, sinking down into it with a sigh.

"You handled that perfectly," he said, sitting back down too.

She shook her head slightly, as though dismissing his words. "I have personal experience with a similar situation. My cousin and her husband were like Mr. and Mrs. Watkiss. They were on completely different pages about their son's treatment and the potential outcome. No middle ground, at all. And once his father shut down and stopped being involved, things became precarious, including young Colin's medical care at home."

Of course, that was what she'd meant when she'd mentioned Tamika's long-term health earlier. Irrespective of whether the young woman got a transplant or not, she was going to need support to make sure she adhered to her medical regimen. If her parents divorced, the stability of her home life and support system would be eroded. Not to mention the emotional toll it would take.

"Was that the cousin whose son needed bone marrow?"

She nodded and rubbed the back of her neck. "The marriage ended even before Colin died."

There was sadness in her tone, and compassion, and it moved him. There was something so steady about her, so intelligent and caring.

David heard himself say, "Have dinner with me this evening."

Her eyes widened slightly, and in the harsh office lights he could swear the color of her irises changed. Deepened. Then she shook her head and reached to pull a file folder closer on her desk.

"I'm afraid I can't. I have a prior engagement."

She'd said she lived alone, but that didn't preclude a boyfriend. In fact, he'd be surprised if she were single.

Before he could comment further, she lifted her chin and met his gaze, her expression somehow forbidding.

"To be honest, even if I didn't, I still would hesitate to be seen with you outside of the hospital. You have the type of high profile that seems to always make your movements of interest to the press, and since we work together, that might call my reputation into question."

Startled, he was about to argue but realized she was right. Especially now, with his push to make Rally Round a success, he was back once more in the public eye and had been the focus of the paparazzi. Almost every day there were articles in the papers, not just about the rally but with the old, dredged-up stories.

Realistically, he should be relieved by her refusal, but instead it made his nerves tingle and threw him back behind the stiff, curt facade that was now second nature.

"Very well," he said, getting to his feet and nodding her way. "Good afternoon. I'll see you tomorrow morning, when we start the testing on Tamika."

Then, he left before he could make a bigger idiot of himself.

CHAPTER SIX

THE MORNING AFTER the meeting between her, Mr. Watkiss, and David, Val was at work earlier than usual. Considering the debacle of the previous morning, she decided to leave home with plenty of time to deal with any mishaps that might occur on her commute.

Of course, because of that, she got to the hospital in good time, but it was just as well. Having David Kennedy around the day before had completely thrown her off her stride, and there was a backlog of work on her desk.

It would be easier to get through the paperwork if she weren't so tired, she thought, rubbing her eyes. But sleep had been elusive the night before and, when it had come, fractured by dreams. Misty imaginings in which David figured all too prominently and that awoke a long-dormant sensuality in her, leaving her shaken and aroused on waking.

Leaving work the evening before, she'd hoped to forget about David, at least for a little while, but that wasn't to be. It was immediately obvious that Emma was a great fan of his, and she insisted on speaking about him in glowing terms the entire time they were together trying on the clothes she'd amassed.

"He's a really nice man," she said. "And was amazing to work for. It was because of him that I got interested in the entire area of transplantation."

By the end of the night, Val knew far more about David Kennedy than she wanted—at least that was what she told herself—and much of it seemed incompatible with the cool, arrogant man she'd met.

"He adopted his son, Josh, after marrying the boy's mum and, when Georgie died, raised him by himself. David never knew his father, so when Sir Arthur died and left David all his money, it was a circus, but David rode it out with class. I admire him so much," she concluded, seemingly unaware of how quiet Val was.

Val wished she could say she wasn't interested in what Emma had to say about David, but in fact it was the complete opposite. No matter how she told herself she wasn't intrigued by him, there was a real thirst on her part to know more about the infuriating ex-surgeon.

She'd said the first thing that came to mind when he'd invited her out to dinner, but it was only a part of why she'd refused.

Looking back, she couldn't recall ever having the kind of visceral reaction to any other man she'd met, and it frankly scared her half to death. Although she was honest enough to admit a part of her was gratified by his apparent interest, she also couldn't help wondering *why* he'd asked her out to dinner.

Was it just an impulse on his part? Had she misinterpreted, and it was, in reality, a working dinner he'd been after?

Surely the intense attraction she felt wasn't reciprocal?

She shook her head, even while her skin tingled and warmth settled low in her belly, as she remembered the sexy dreams she'd had last night.

There was no way a man as gorgeous as David Kennedy, who could have any woman he crooked a finger at, could be as drawn to her as she was to him.

"Damn it," she grumbled, disheartened and even more distracted, and annoyed at herself for it. "I don't have time for this."

But, try as she might, she couldn't get her brain to focus on the task at hand so she eventually closed the file in front of her and got up from her desk.

Luckily, she didn't have any reason to interact with Dr. Kennedy that day, as he'd be busy supervising Tamika's tests. Having looked at the schedule the afternoon before, she knew he wasn't due into the hospital until ten so she decided to check on Tamika before he arrived.

Hopefully a walk would help to clear her head and maybe even evict David Kennedy from it.

She should have known that wouldn't be her lot. Before she could even leave her office, her phone rang.

"Val." Emma sounded rushed. "Have you given any more thought to being involved in the documentary? I promised David I'd get back to him today."

To hell with David Kennedy.

The words not only crossed her mind but threatened to come out of her mouth too. Val bit them back just in time.

"I think you'll bring a different and important perspective to the conversation," Emma went on, before Val could answer. "But it's completely up to you, of course."

When Emma had mentioned it the night before, her enthusiasm had been obvious, but Val was more cautious by nature and had asked for time to sleep on it. Having the rally filmed with a variety of people interviewed would definitely amplify the message they were trying to send, but still Val found herself hesitating.

Was that out of annoyance with David, or did she have a deeper reason to want to refuse?

Realizing it was the former, she shook her head at her own foolishness and said, "Yes, I'll do it."

"Wonderful," Emma replied. "Have to run. I'll talk to you soon."

At the elevator, Val pushed the button, as she stuck her phone back into her pocket and contemplated how much bigger Rally Round was turning out to be than she'd expected.

Originally it was billed as a two-week fun run, with stops along the way where participants could talk to locals. A week ago, after hearing increasing buzz about it, she'd gone back to the website and had been shocked at the increased scope. Not only were there hospitals and transplant teams involved, but a wide variety of foundations, research laboratories, and even the blood banks. The number of outreach events had increased too, and the places listed as the venues were large convention centers.

Obviously they were expecting crowds of people.

If they got them, it would be all for the better. The message they were trying to impart—that donors of all ethnicities and types were desperately needed—was important. And the setup of the events, where medical professionals were able to actually talk to the public in a casual, less stressful setting, was brilliant.

No matter how else she felt about David, she had to admit he'd come up with a masterful plan. Whether it would have the hoped-for effect was left to be seen.

When she got to Tamika's room, she found the young woman with her breakfast in front of her but her complete and total concentration focused on the TV rather than her meal.

Then Val heard the voice coming out of the television, and her heart flipped over.

"Rally Round is aimed at informing the public about the work medical teams do to improve quality of life for many patients through transplants, research, and therapies."

Val looked at the screen, and there he was—David Kennedy, dressed in another impeccable suit, speaking in that cool, autocratic way he had, about his pet project.

Tearing her eyes away from the TV, Val said, "Tamika, eat your breakfast."

"Mm-hmm," she mumbled, reaching for her toast, gaze still glued on the morning show. "Dr. David's much nicer in person than he seems on TV, don't you think?"

Maybe to you!

But even as Val thought it, she knew it wasn't fair. She'd seen him with his mask off, and Tamika was right.

Or was the kindly, concerned face he showed his patients and their families the mask, and the cool arrogance his real personality?

The female host smiled, and asked, "So the rally is aimed at transplant awareness? If so, how do blood services come into it?"

David's eyebrows twitched, as though the question was ridiculous, but replied, "Without blood donations, most surgeons can't operate on their patients. There are also a host of diseases that require frequent blood transfusions as part of a course of treatment."

He sat forward slightly, and the camera closed in on him. A shiver ran down Val's spine, as she remembered him kneeling at her feet, his fingers tender on her skin.

When he spoke, it was in the same cool, controlled tone, but she could see the determination in his gaze. "While the rally concept started as a way to highlight the important work transplant teams and researchers are doing, it's morphed into something even more important. It is an opportunity to explain to people just how important they—the public—are in regard to the work we all do. Without donors, much of what we do would be impossible. There are thousands of people on waiting lists who could be helped if their friends, families, neighbors, everyone signed up to be tested or added their names to the donor lists."

The morning show host nodded, as though in agreement, but prompted, "I'm sure that's true, but not everyone is willing to be a donor, are they?"

"No." Val was sure the temperature in the studio must have fallen a few degrees, his voice was so frosty. "And there are some people who can't volunteer to be a donor because of their own health struggles or for religious reasons. But for the thousands who can, even if they don't like the idea of being an organ donor, they may be able to donate blood."

The male host started speaking, but his voice was drowned out by the sound of something crashing to the floor off-screen and the hullabaloo that followed.

"What—?"

Before Tamika could say anything more, a blur of fuzz dashed onto the set and, in a flash, jumped into David Kennedy's lap.

"Oh, Lord," Tamika hooted. "It's one of the dogs from the next segment! They said they were going to show some shelter animals up for adoption."

The consternation the escapee pup had caused continued unabated for a couple seconds, with the morning show hosts laughing and someone off-camera hissing frantically, "Gryphon! Gryphon, come!"

David had a look of such comical surprise on his face that Val couldn't help chuckling. Then, as though he'd heard her, David started laughing too.

Val's amusement dried up as a heated wave rushed over her skin. The deep, melodic sound of his delight seemed to vibrate right into her bones and strike lightning out into every nook and cranny of her body.

She'd heard him express amusement before, but never like this—head thrown back to avoid the dog's kisses, laughing freely, his eyes sparkling.

He was beautiful, and she wanted him at that moment more than she'd ever wanted anything—anyone—in her life.

"I'm so sorry." The dog handler sidled into view and reached for the leash attached to her runaway's collar. "So sorry. Let me—"

"No. No." David waved her back, settling the dog more firmly on his lap. "He's fine here. I think he came over to remind me that dogs and cats sometimes need transfusions too, so if you have an animal who's healthy and robust, you can speak to your vet and ask about blood donorship."

"On that note, I'll say thank you to Dr. Kennedy and to Gryphon," the other host said, just as the camera zoomed in on man and dog.

Hearing his name, the dog paused in his continued attempt to lick David's face and stared straight at the host, one ear up and the other down, his expression one of adorable inquiry and unmistakable mischief. The theme music started playing, and over it, before they went to commercial, Val could hear someone once more apologizing to David and his responding laughter.

"Aww, so cute," Tamika said.

Unsure of whether she was referring to dog or man, Val expressed no opinion but reminded the young woman to finish up her breakfast.

"Did you know Dr. David's mum is a singer?" Tamika asked, around a mouthful of toast and egg. "Or that he never knew who his father was until he died and left him a ton of money?"

"I did," Val replied, silently wondering why she couldn't seem to escape people speaking about the dratted man.

"And that his wife died young and his son is her son that he adopted?"

"Did you find all that out during his TV interview?" she asked rather than replying to the question.

"No. They were mostly only interested in that rally thing Dr. David is doing now. I looked him up on the internet, after my mum said his mum was the one who sang my Gran's favorite song." She paused with her fork partway to her mouth and asked, "Did you know he's putting on that rally?"

"I did," Val said again. "You hadn't heard about it before?"

Talking about the rally would be a lot easier than having to hear even more about the man she was trying so hard not to think about.

"No. I don't usually watch the news or those morning shows. I only watched today because I heard Dr. David's name as I was changing channels. Are you going to be at some of the information events where people can sign up to be donors?"

"Better than that. I'll be driving in the rally with my friend, Emma."

Tamika's eyes widened. "Ooh, you're so lucky. I wish I could too. He said it was starting in Edinburgh and ending in London. Do you know what the route will be? And what did he mean when he said there would be a gimmick component to it? Isn't a rally just cars racing as fast as they can from one place to another?"

Val shook her head, smiling over Tamika's obvious enthusiasm.

"No, you're thinking of WRC rallies, like you see on TV, where the cars are all going hell-for-leather along the road, jumping over humps and skidding around corners. This rally is what they call a TSD—time, speed, distance—rally. That means the cars have to go a specific distance, within a specific time, while maintaining or even going under the speed limit."

Tamika wrinkled her nose. "That doesn't sound like as much fun as the fast races."

Val chuckled. "Sometimes TSD rallies will have special stages, where the drivers can go as fast as they like, but because the cars in this rally are all older, there won't be any of those."

"Still sounds like fun, even if you're not really racing."

That made Val laugh. "Hey, it's still a race, even if we're not driving fast. If you get lost or don't follow the directions, you'll lose."

"I guess. But what about the gimmick part? What's that?"

"I'm not sure what the gimmick part of it will be. Sometimes you have to look out for special signs along the way and if you see them all you get points, or it could be something completely different. The folks at Rally Round have kept that part of it under their hats, but you could look that up online and see what rally clubs have done before. And, to answer your other question, drivers and navigators never know what the route is until the start of each day, so they can't cheat and check it out beforehand."

"Maybe I can get Dad to take me to see the cars, if you're coming near here."

The longing in her voice was heartbreaking, but Val smiled and kept her voice light as she replied, "And you can watch some of it on TV. They're having daily coverage, taping interviews, and even doing a documentary to air afterwards. I think some of the information is on the Rally Round website."

"Will you be in the documentary?"

Before Val could answer, the door opened, and one of the nurses came in.

"Finished your breakfast yet? It'll soon be time to take you to radiology."

Which meant David Kennedy would soon be putting in an appearance. Val wasn't going to stick around for that!

"I'll see you later, Tamika."

"All right, Mrs. Sterling."

Making her escape, knowing that there was no way David could make it from the TV studio to the hospital in such a short period of time, Val couldn't help glancing around. Although, it was impossible to decide whether she was hoping to see him or avoid him.

That afternoon, as she was doing her rounds of patients she was working with and heard Dr. Kennedy had been called away back to London, she tried to tell herself she was relieved.

Even as she recognized the lie for what it was.

CHAPTER SEVEN

EIGHT DAYS REALLY wasn't enough to get her equilibrium back, but it was all the time Val got before David Kennedy came back into her life. Returning to her office after a meeting, she opened her calendar to see an appointment with him and the Watkiss family for that afternoon. Heart pounding, her face ablaze from the warmth rushing through her veins, she called through to Shala to ask who had made the arrangements.

"Dr. Kennedy's PA called to say she'd set up the appointment with Mrs. Watkiss, and Dr. Kennedy asked her to find out if you were available to sit in. The PA apologized for the short notice, saying it was the only time Dr. Kennedy could fit them in, but I didn't think you'd mind since you were free anyway."

It was on the tip of Val's tongue to tell Shala the damned man could have simple set up a video conference call rather than have everyone running about after him, but she bit back the words. After all, it wasn't Shala's fault Val's system had instantly gone into a crazy type of hyperdrive just from seeing the doctor's name.

With only about two weeks before the rally, one would think he'd be too busy to be traveling around, but even as she huffed in annoyance, she admired his commitment to Tamika's case. She just wished knowing about his upcoming visit to the hospital didn't make her feel as though she was suddenly on quicksand.

Thank goodness she had a bit of time before they were scheduled to meet, and if she timed it perfectly, they'd spend no time alone beforehand.

Preferably not afterward either.

Leaning back in her chair, she tried to get her breathing and heart rate under control, mystified by her reactions to David Kennedy. She wasn't the type to get all giddy about a man—never had been. Even as a young woman, her approach to the opposite sex had been more prosaic than anything else. And she was far from young now, with harsh experience to tell her not to let hormones take over her brain, so feeling this way was ridiculous, wasn't it? Especially about someone she had to work with, and who was fathoms out of her league.

Then it struck her that, under normal circumstances, she'd be informed what decision a consulting doctor had come to prior to the meeting, so she could be prepared. A quick scan of her email showed no such message, and although there were a few handwritten slips on her desk, none of them were from David.

Now, she was just annoyed, and thankful for that emotion, since it allowed her to focus on his ill manners rather than his other, more attractive, attributes.

Yet, even so, it took a concerted effort—and giving herself a stern talking-to—for her to settle down and actually begin to get work done.

Just as she'd started, Shala rang through from reception.

"Mrs. Sterling, Dr. Kennedy wonders if he could speak to you?"

About time.

Although it was about an hour before the meeting with the Watkiss family, at least he was deigning to clue her in to what was happening!

"Yes," she said, the receiver in a death grip, as she waited for Shala to put him through. When the phone clicked as though the call was cut off, she thought Shala had disconnected it by accident and was totally unprepared to see her door open and David step into her office.

He was clearly on his cellular phone—just not with her.

"Just a moment," he said, touching the earpiece in his right ear. "I'm sorry, Mrs. Sterling, but do you mind if I finish my conversation in here?"

"Not at all," she replied, flustered and feeling silly to be caught with her receiver still in her hand. As she put it back on the base, she added, "Do you need some privacy? I could step out…"

"No, no." Clearly distracted, he shook his head and murmured, "Excuse me," before walking over to the only window in the room and returning to his call.

His preoccupation with what the person on the other end was saying allowed Val to watch him freely, and she took full advantage. He looked different, but it was a few moments before she realized why.

There was a slightly disheveled air about him, in contrast to his usual crisp, sartorial elegance. Instead of a full tailored suit, he was wearing just dress pants and a light blue shirt, the sleeves of which were rolled up, revealing strong forearms. As she watched he reached up and, with a jerk, loosened the knot of his tie, the motion one of terse annoyance.

"I will not be in London on that day, as you well know," he said coldly, the fingers of one hand clenching into a fist on the windowsill. "I will be in Edinburgh for the drivers' meeting prior to the start of the rally."

Whatever the person on the other end of the line said in reply had his eyes narrowing and made his lips tighten into a straight, hard line.

"Perhaps you're unfamiliar with the bylaws governing the matter, but I'm afraid your discomfort isn't one of the few reasons listed for calling an extraordinary board meeting. The only alternative would be a greater-than-two-thirds majority of members agreeing to meet, and you will *not* get that."

While his body language was tense—angry— his voice had been so controlled that the emphasis on that one word cracked like a whip, making Val start. She might have felt sorry for the other person, except she realized that beneath David's so tightly controlled anger lay something else.

Was it fear?

As he silently listened to whatever was being said by the other person, David lightly tapped his fist on the windowsill, which Val interpreted as further evidence of his reined-in fury.

"If you wish to waste time on attempting to sabotage the rally, causing embarrassment, and making the foundation lose more of the very money you say I'm wasting, I wish you luck. I have an appointment with a patient, so good day, Malcolm."

He disconnected the call, taking the earbud out and stuffing it into his pocket, but he didn't turn away from the window. Instead, he stood there for a few moments, staring out, his lips twisting slightly as though his thoughts were less than pleasant.

Then he turned to face Val and said, "So how is *your* day going?"

And, just like that, all she could see was the

weariness behind his determinedly smiling demeanor, and something inside her melted.

"Better than yours, I wager, from the sounds of it," she replied, her tone far gentler than any she usually used at work.

Right before her eyes that air of good humor drained away, leaving him shaking his head as he strode over to the chair on the other side of her desk and dropped into it.

"One of the GDK directors is trying to make trouble and turn the rally into a public-relations fiasco. If he could, he'd have the entire thing canceled."

Surprised both by his statement and his candor, Val leaned back in her chair. "Why would he do something like that? It would ruin or at the very least damage the foundation's reputation."

There was still anger in his expression, but mostly David just looked exhausted.

"He believes that the money we're spending on the rally is being wasted and would be better served elsewhere."

Val couldn't help giving a snort of amusement, although there was nothing amusing about the situation at all. "Doesn't he know that the money used to set up the foundation was yours?"

The look her gave her was searching, as though he was considering what he should say, and then he sighed, one shoulder rising and falling in a shrug.

"I made sure to set up the foundation so that no matter what might happen to me, it would be able to continue on, unaffected, run by the board of directors. I approached Sir Malcolm Hypolite to be a director, knowing he had been closely involved with heart-transplant research in the past. Unfortunately, unbeknownst to me, he'd been a good friend of Sir Arthur Knutson."

He hesitated for an instant, glancing down at his hands before continuing. "My father. Even after fifteen years, Malcolm still seems to think of the foundation's money as belonging to Sir Arthur and feels I'm some type of interloper who had little to no right to the funds to begin with."

He said it casually, but somehow now she was able to see beyond the mask he usually wore around her to the man who'd gone through more than most people could even imagine. She found herself wanting to ease the strain she could see in his gaze and lighten the atmosphere.

"Fifteen years, you say? Apparently, Sir Malcolm is a slow learner, hmm?"

And his burst of laughter made her almost ridiculously happy.

The last thing David thought he'd be doing that day was having a moment of levity with Val Sterling. He'd been in turns angry with her and with himself, since under normal circumstances this trip to Liverpool would have been nothing more strenuous than a conference call. Yet, here he was, all because he couldn't get the woman seated across the desk from him out of his head.

In the midst of all he had going on, constantly thinking about Val had caused his already sky-high stress levels to become stratospheric. Even though she'd already told him she wouldn't go out with him, and knowing he really didn't have time to do anything about the attraction, he'd known he had to see her again.

Trying to convince himself to wait until the rally didn't fly.

Neither did the long days of work, which should have left him too tired to even consider driving the almost three hours from his home in Oxfordshire back to St. Agnes Hospital. And even the myriad tasks he could achieve in the time he was wasting making the trip somehow didn't seem important.

All he wanted was to see Val again—a need that left him feeling ridiculously juvenile.

So, instead of concentrating on Rally Round and all of the other million issues on his agenda, he was seated in her office, basking in the smile she was sending his way.

And speaking to her about things he would normally never discuss with anyone.

There was something so honest and straightforward about her that he instinctively trusted her.

In response to what she'd said about Malcolm,

he replied, "A slow learner or, at the very least, tenacious."

"Ahh," she said, still smiling and nodding slowly. "So *tenacious* is the latest synonym for *bloody-minded*, is it? Fifteen years is definitely too long even for tenacity. You'd think he'd have moved on by now."

David leaned back, feeling much of the stress he was carrying in his shoulders ease. "You would think so, wouldn't you? To her credit, right after I was informed about the inheritance, my mother did try to warn me it might happen, in her euphemistic way."

"Oh?" Val's eyebrows rose. "What did she say?"

"'Dahling, there may be some people who'll be a teensy bit upset when this gets out.'"

Val snorted, and he wasn't sure if it was because of his mother's words or his drawling impersonation.

"Your mum is a master of understatement, I see."

"My mum doesn't like to discuss anything that she deems *unpleasant* and, rather than speak the truth, would prefer to hide behind smiles and laughter."

The old bitterness was still there, tempered by life and the passage of time, yet by no means gone or forgotten.

Val seemed to hear it and tilted her head slightly,

those remarkable eyes searching his face as though looking for passage to his soul.

"You don't get on with your mother?"

Normally he would have withdrawn from the conversation long before this point, ducking behind the barriers he used for protection, both of his privacy and his pride. But somehow, with Val, he was comfortable enough to say, "We're cordial, but it's never been the same since the truth about my father came out."

Now her brow wrinkled. "Why?"

This was new territory. He'd never spoken to anyone about the time right after being informed by the attorneys that he'd inherited Sir Arthur's considerable fortune. Shell-shocked, still grieving Georgie's death, he'd gone to his mother for clarity and comfort and received even more shocking news.

"I was angry when I discovered she'd been in touch with Sir Arthur over all the intervening years but never told me, even when I'd become an adult."

The coolness was creeping back into his tone, but a dam had broken inside, and he couldn't seem to stop talking.

"When I was a child, I'd ask her about my father, and she'd say things like 'Don't worry about him' or 'He doesn't matter' or 'Aren't I enough?' effectively guilting me into not asking anymore."

Restless energy made him want to get up and

pace, but he forced himself to stay where he was, although he couldn't stop himself from shifting in his seat.

"Did you ever wonder why?"

If she'd sounded as if she were sorry for him, or even too avidly interested, David might have found the impetus to stop, but her voice was as calm as ever.

"I thought maybe he was some kind of gangster, and she was afraid. Or, when I got older and realized she never stuck to one man for long, I wondered if it were a case that she didn't know who my father was or if I were the product of an assault. To find out that she was in constant contact with the man who'd fathered me but she didn't even allow me to meet him…"

He didn't want to talk about how painful that had been, or how, even now, just saying it out loud opened a cold void in his belly.

"Did she tell you why?"

"As I said, she's not one to talk about anything unpleasant."

"Is that what you really think was stopping her?"

"No. I think she was protecting Sir Arthur—his reputation and standing in society."

Val leaned forward, placing her elbows on her desk and rubbing the fisted fingers of one hand slowly under her nose, her deeply contemplative gaze affixed to his.

"What?" he asked, self-conscious under that silent perusal. "If you're hesitating to say what's on your mind, just spit it out."

"I just wondered if you mightn't have it backward," she said slowly, "and that the person your mother was trying to protect was you."

CHAPTER EIGHT

DAVID WAS STARING at her as though she'd slapped him, and Val felt a searing wave wash over her face. Yet, having come this far, why turn back?

"Think about what you went through after news got out that Sir Arthur was your father and that he'd left you all his money and property. His family set out to vilify you and your mother. Do you think it would have been any different if you were a child?"

"I don't know," he said, in that cold, lazy way he had of speaking, but she wasn't fooled by it anymore. Not now, when she recognized it for the defense mechanism it obviously was. "But she could have told me at any time between childhood and when he died."

Val shook her head, her heart aching. "We're both parents, David, and know how tough a job it is. Worse when you're a single parent, facing myriad decisions that will affect your children and having to make them alone. It's a juggling act."

His face softened slightly, and he slowly nodded. "That I do understand. After my wife died, I second-guessed everything, wondering constantly if I was doing the right thing for Josh."

"Exactly, but raising my boys after their father walked out on us, I faced a heartbreaking dilemma: What do I tell them about their father when he's done something hurtful? How do I react when they're upset because he said he was going to do something and didn't? Or explain why he left in the first place, without making him out to be a horrid person?"

David opened his mouth as though to respond, but she raised her hand, letting him know she wasn't finished.

"Think how much more tolerant people are now about mixed-race relationships and babies born out of wedlock in comparison to fifty years ago, when you were born. Imagine your mum wondering what making your paternity known might do to her career and how it might affect you both in the short and long term. And maybe back then your father had to wonder about his career too. Yes, he came from a wealthy family, but from what I've heard, he forged his own path in life also. Perhaps he figured you'd be better off without his acknowledgment while he was still alive, but at least he remembered you—acknowledged paternity—when he died."

"That's all well and good, but I would have

preferred to at least get to know him, even a little, while he was alive." The sound he made was undecipherable, but it made the ache around Val's heart deepen. "I was going to refuse the inheritance, let his nieces and nephews have it, but I was too angry to, especially when they started slandering my mother and me. How could any of that be better or worse than if my parents had been honest from the beginning?"

Val lifted her hands, signaling her understanding of how helpless he must have felt. "I can't hazard a guess as to what was going through your parents' minds at any point in time. And, realistically, if your mum doesn't want to talk about it, you may never know the truth either. But don't you think it's time you put that part of your life to rest rather than let it color your relationship with her? Having just lost my mother not too long ago, my advice to you is to treasure the time you have left, so you and Josh fully enjoy her while you can."

"Josh has a great relationship with her," he replied, but the words sounded automatic, and his voice was quiet, almost introspective. "And it's not as though we're always fighting."

He fell silent, and Val left him to his thoughts, hoping he would at least consider what she'd said. Having lost her father at a young age and nursed her mother through her long illness, Val was well aware of the value of family. Even though she'd been hurt when Liam had moved out to live with Des, she'd maintained contact as best she could with her son. No matter how fraught the relationship was, it was no reason to lose the connection she had with her youngest.

"Why did he leave?"

Startled, Val looked up to find David's gaze intent on her face.

"I'm sorry, what?"

"Your husband. Why did he leave?"

It was on the tip of her tongue to tell him to mind his own business, but what actually came out was, "My mother had MS and couldn't manage on her own anymore. I told Des I wanted her to come and live with us, and he told me it was her or him." She lifted her chin, to show she had no regrets. "It should have been a far harder decision than it was, but although my ex-husband pretended to be the consummate family man, once he showed his true colors, it was easy. Instead of Mum coming to Newcastle to live with us, I packed up the boys and moved in with her in Scotland, and we lived there until she died, eight months ago."

"I'm sorry for your loss," he said, and somehow, she knew he really meant it and wasn't just mouthing platitudes. There was a wealth of understanding about grief in those simple words. "Emma had mentioned you looked after her father before he died, and I assumed it was in a hospital or long-term facility. Now you have me wondering how you managed with your sons and mother and full-time work too."

Easier now, to move to something a bit less personal—and painful.

"I left my hospital job when Mum needed additional care and was lucky enough to be able to do some home-care work, so I could be nearby and have a more flexible schedule. Mr. Owen was one of my patients, and he was a lovely man. We used to talk about all kinds of things. He was an archeologist and had traveled extensively and loved cars. My brother was into anything with an engine so we had that in common too."

"Which is how Emma knew to invite you to navigate for her in the rally." It was a statement rather than a question, so she just nodded. "Are you looking forward to it?"

Casual conversation, but there was an undercurrent that had Val's skin prickling with awareness and made the complex attraction she felt for him come sharply back into focus.

"I am." Strange how her brain, which moments before had been completely clear and focused, seemed to get foggy, so that she wasn't paying attention to what she was saying. "I've been wanting a bit of an adventure, and I think the rally will do nicely."

His eyelids dipped, not as though he were looking down but as if shielding the expression in his eyes. Her heart rate accelerated, and her body reacted as though touched, as she shivered with the knowledge that this was a man who could tie her in knots without even trying.

If she allowed him to.

Before either of them could say another word, the phone on her desk rang, and Val hastened to answer it.

"Yes, Shala?"

"Dr. Laghari is wondering if you have a minute."

Remembering the previous misunderstanding, she asked, "Is he out there?"

"No," came the reply, in a surprised tone. "On the phone, of course."

"Put him through, please." Covering the mouthpiece, she said to David, "It's Dr. Laghari, no doubt wondering if I've heard anything about your decision regarding Tamika."

"If her parents agree, I think she's a good candidate for the transplant list."

She tried to rein in her instinctive joy and remain professional but knew she'd done a poor job of it when David nodded and smiled back at her.

David watched Val as she spoke to Dr. Laghari on the phone, his thoughts not on the patient who'd ostensibly brought him to Liverpool but on the conversation they'd just shared.

What was it about this woman that led him to open up to her in such a way?

And how was she able to cut through years of anger and pain and resentment with a kind of common sense he was kicking himself for not having from the start?

His only excuse was that he'd been in the thick of it all those years ago and had been functioning solely on the need to survive—and to care for Josh too. Rage and grief had helped him get through it and, somewhere along the line, he'd forgotten to let them go.

Now, it felt as though a burden he hadn't even realized he was carrying had lifted, and he owed that to Val.

She hung up the phone, and he could see she'd pulled her businesslike cloak around herself once more by the way she pulled the file on her desk closer and laid her hands on it. But he wasn't ready to let go of the intimacy they'd shared quite yet.

Before she could speak, he said, "Thank you."

Surprise had her eyebrows going up. "For?"

"Being so sensible and showing me that I was being as bad as Malcolm—holding on to a grudge I should have abandoned a long time ago."

She shrugged and looked down but couldn't hide the pink blush that touched her cheeks.

"You're welcome, but I think you'd have figured it out yourself, eventually."

"You're too kind." He couldn't help chuckling, although the moment felt too heavy for levity. "After saying Malcolm was a slow learner, I'd have expected the same criticism."

When she looked up, he was surprised to see what appeared to be a sheen of tears in her eyes.

"It's harder to see these things when you're in the middle of them and they bring you genuine pain." Then she shook her head and smiled slightly. "The situation with your father's estate is none of Sir Malcolm's business. He's just *being* a pain."

He couldn't help laughing and watched in delight as she laughed too. Then, wanting to test the limits of this new phase of their relationship, he said, "I know you don't want to be seen with me, but I'd like to see you, outside of the hospital."

Expecting her to immediately turn him down, he was surprised when she didn't answer and another wave of pink tinged her face.

"I don't think that would be a good idea."

But there was no conviction in her voice, and he couldn't suppress the wave of triumph that sliced through his system.

"Think about it," he said. "And let me know if you're interested in a different type of adventure. No pressure," he added, as it looked as though she were going to refuse outright. "I have to drive back to Oxfordshire after our meeting anyway."

"You do know you could have just set up a

conference call instead of coming all this way, right?"

In for a penny, in for a pound.

"Yes, but I wanted to see you again."

Her eyes widened and darkened, and he wanted to kiss her in that moment more than he wanted his next breath.

Then she looked away, glancing at her watch, but she licked her lips before saying in a voice that probably wasn't as brisk as she would have liked it to be, "The Watkisses will be here soon."

With a sigh and a nod, he reached up to straighten his tie, lifting his collar to make sure it was properly centered, as Val got up to go to her filing cabinet.

While she was walking back to her seat, she said, "Your collar is sticking up a bit at the side."

"This one?" he asked, fumbling a little.

"No," she replied. "Here, let me…"

Then she was beside him, her fingers brushing his neck as she got his collar settled and, not one to pass up an opportunity, he caught her fingers in his and pulled them gently to his lips.

He'd meant to kiss the back of her hand only but couldn't help touching his lips to her fingers too. Her hand trembled in his, and her indrawn gasp was unmistakably one of pleasure rather than censure, and she didn't pull away. So he turned her hand over and kissed her fingertips and then her palm.

And letting her go was the hardest thing he could remember doing in forever, but he forced himself to do it anyway.

"Think about it," he said again, looking up into her rapt face, his voice raspy with longing. "Please."

And then had to leave it at that as her phone rang and she hurried back to the other side of the desk, leaving him to try and steady his racing heart and put on his doctor hat before the patient and her family arrived.

CHAPTER NINE

VAL FELT AS though she could hardly catch her breath as she tried to compose herself before the Watkiss family got to her office.

David Kennedy had turned her inside out with just the lightest of touches—his lips on her hand—and she wasn't sure how she hadn't spontaneously combusted.

Think about it.

His words echoed in her head until she could hardly bear it, since she knew she'd be thinking about little else for a very long time.

The simmering tension between them was both sexual and something deeper, and all of it was scary.

Her every reaction to him said David could easily wrap her up emotionally as well as physically, and that was a road she didn't want to go down.

Whatever this was brewing and simmering between them couldn't last. She wouldn't let it. After meeting him and becoming insatiably curious, she'd read everything she could find on the internet about his life. It had been illuminating, and a little overawing, but certain things stuck out to her, when looking at the articles.

First was the pain and heartache he'd gone through—something he'd confirmed during their conversation. No amount of money in the world could make up for not knowing his father, losing his wife at such a young age, or being alienated from his mother.

With the threat of MS hanging over her, she had no intention of inflicting that kind of uncertainty on anyone else, so a relationship with David or any other man was out of the question.

She also had a difficult time comprehending the media bubble he'd existed in since his inheritance. One he seemed quite happy to inhabit. Just the thought of constantly being under prying eyes filled Val with horror.

She had learned the hard way what could happen when a relationship fell apart and outsiders got involved. Where she'd lived during her marriage in Newcastle was like a village within the city. It seemed like almost before she and Des had decided to part ways, everyone was talking about it and taking sides. Pride dictated Val not talk to anyone about what was going on, but Des had no such qualms and had made her out to be the villain. It had been a relief to leave, just to get away from the wagging tongues.

The ordeal—having the father of her children spread lies about her, just to make sure no one thought him the bad guy—had left her scarred and mistrustful. How much worse would it be if she'd been involved with a high-profile individual, like David Kennedy?

No, that was an additional complication she neither wanted nor needed.

But with the way her body came alive around him, reminding her she was once a sensual woman with robust needs and desires, if he offered a no-strings affair? That, she thought, suppressing a little shiver of longing, was something she would certainly consider.

If, just a week ago, anyone had suggested she indulge in a hot, sexy encounter, she'd have scoffed. Not that she didn't like sex. She'd liked it a lot when she was younger, before the pressures of life had made it seem unimportant and not worth the bother.

But now she was thinking she'd happily bother for David Kennedy.

Just the thought made her want to squirm and had her forcing her brain to abandon such thoughts so she could focus on the meeting about to start.

The consultation with the Watkiss family went better than Val expected. It quickly became apparent that Tamika, Ricardo, and Lena Watkiss had finally had a heart-to-heart and now were on the same page.

When David advised them that he was recommending Tamika go on the list, all three of them nodded, and it was her father who replied.

"All right. Put her on the list, please." The trepidation was still in his eyes, but he was holding his wife's hand. Mrs. Watkiss dabbed at her damp cheeks, even though she was also beaming. "And we'll take it a day at a time."

"Dr. David, I want to help with Rally Round." Tamika's tone was serious and far too mature for her age. "I think you should have them interview me, so people can see the real diversity of people needing transplants. That's part of what your rally is all about, isn't it?"

"It is. But are you sure that's something you want to do? Believe me, being in the spotlight isn't always a good thing."

She shrugged, her expression solemn. "I don't care who knows what's happening to me, but you're the one who said on the TV that there's a real need for minority communities to realize how many of their own are in need. Do you already have someone of Caribbean descent in your documentary?"

"I don't think so. I'd have to check with the producers."

"Well, if you don't, I'll do it."

David looked at her parents and asked if they

would be willing to sign off on her participation, and both of them agreed.

"I'll get back to you about it, but please, remember being a part of the documentary won't necessarily improve your chances of finding a donor."

Tamika nodded. "You've told us my chances are small already, but I couldn't help thinking that there are a lot more people like me out there, in the same boat, you know? Whose families came here from somewhere else, and they need their community to get involved." Then she gave that cheeky grin that never failed to make Val smile, even as its bravado broke her heart just a little too. "Besides, I'm cute and still a child. People go gaga over cute kids, don't they?"

David laughed and agreed. "Yes, they definitely do."

Then, far sooner than Val was prepared for, the meeting was over, the Watkisses were taking their leave, and she was walking them out. She reiterated that she would be sending them paperwork to sign, but her mind was already cycling back to David, who had made no move to leave her office.

After she closed the door behind the departing family, she hesitated for a moment, taking a deep breath before turning to face him.

And promptly lost the air from her lungs all over again.

There it was again. That hooded gaze that made her knees wobbly and had all kinds of erotic, chaotic thoughts running through her head.

"This is crazy."

She hadn't meant to say it aloud, but heard the words as though from a distance.

"I agree," he replied, his voice so low and deep she could swear she felt it in her bones. "There's no denying there's something between us, but I'm not sure what to do about it."

There was desire there but also confusion and what she could only interpret as frustration too, and it had her crossing the room before she'd thought it through.

Then it was too late, because he took her in his arms, and that gorgeous, stern mouth was on hers, and there was no space for contemplation—only sensation.

She expected ferocity. After all, the attraction between them felt explosive, and in her experience that should give a frantic edge to this first encounter as the barriers came down. But David didn't take. Instead he seemed on a quest to entice her full, unwavering complicity.

Sipping, tempting, exploring her lips until her entire focus—her being—was centered on where their mouths met. Oh, she was fully aware of the lean, hard length of his body, the strength of his arms, and the luscious scent of him filling her head, but it was his kiss that stole her breath completely. Cracked her inhibitions, then shattered them into tiny pieces, so that she was the one who deepened their kiss and pulled him closer in ever-growing desire.

When her phone rang, it took a long moment to even realize what it was and all her strength to not just ignore it.

David pulled back, and they exchanged a long look. Val was glad to see he was as breathless as she, and the blaze of need in his eyes made her shiver.

He let his arms slide slowly from around her, and she gathered enough strength to walk away, when all she wanted was to stay exactly where she'd been.

By the time she'd dealt with her call, he was standing behind the guest chair, and from his somber expression she knew the interlude was over.

"I have to go."

"Yes." She nodded as though it didn't matter, although inside she was straining toward him, wanting him to stay.

"Val, with the rally and everything else that's going on right now, I don't have the time you deserve me to give you."

"Yes," she said again, although she was thinking *I'll take whatever you want to give* and was despising herself for the impulse.

"Don't do that."

"What?" To salvage her pride, she raised her eyebrows, feigning mildly questioning interest.

He strode around the desk. Swinging her chair around so she faced him, he bent so they were nose to nose.

"Don't pretend you weren't just in my arms, making the most delicious little sounds in the back of your throat as we kissed, seducing me with that sweet, sexy mouth."

She gasped at the rush of renewed arousal his words brought, and he nodded, that erotic, heavy-lidded gaze doing crazy things to her determination not to give in to her own lust.

"We're not kids, Val, and I won't pretend or make believe as though we were. I want you, in my arms, in my bed, but I'm trying to make sure I can treat you with the care and respect you deserve. And if that means waiting until my life slows down, then I'm willing—reluctant, but willing—to do it."

He was melting her, from the inside out, and Val knew she couldn't allow him to do that, yet couldn't seem to stop it from happening. Right then she wanted to resent him. To tell him it wasn't what she wanted and he should just leave—forget it all—but neither the emotion nor the words would come.

Instead, as she sat trapped by his gaze, her body humming as though filled with a million volts of electricity, all she could do was nod silently. That way she wouldn't tell him his high-minded, gentlemanly intentions could go hang, because if he wanted her, she was ready and willing.

"Damn it," he growled. "When you look at me like that—"

Bending, he took her lips. Not gently now but with a driving need that showed her, despite his words, they were actually of the same mind.

But before she could get her arms around his neck, he was pulling away—walking away, with a stiff-backed stride of sheer determination.

Pausing at the door, he looked back to ask, "May I call you later?"

"Yes." As though she could refuse him anything, with her brain still consumed by arousal and her body clamoring for satisfaction.

And when he'd left, closing the door behind him, all Val could do was drop her head down onto her desk, not sure whether to laugh or cry.

David dragged himself back to his car, bogged down not by weariness anymore but by the urge to turn around and go back to Val. To stay in Liverpool and convince her to spend the night with him. But he'd told her the truth when he said he didn't have the time to do right by her. In truth, he barely had time to get the important things in his life done, much less to be contemplating striking up a new relationship.

One that cried out for him to commit to it, the way he did to everything important in his life.

But the commitments he had already shouldered were almost too much, and if he tried to stretch himself any thinner, he might just snap.

If he had any sense at all, he'd walk away altogether and forget about Valerie Sterling.

He considered that idea as he got into his vehicle and put on his seat belt.

Yes, that would be the best course of action. Keep his concentration on the foundation and his work, since those were the most important. Channeling energy into any kind of distraction could cost him everything, and he wasn't willing to pay that price.

And it wasn't as though he were a stranger to having to exert willpower to get what he wanted—which was to ensure what he'd built continued to help as many people as possible.

Navigating through Liverpool, he determinedly turned his thoughts away from Val and back to Rally Round. Using the car's hands-free capability, he put in a call to his PA, Mrs. Rowland.

"Rolly," he said, when she answered the phone. "Do you have any updates for me?"

"Yes, David. Mrs. Duhaney emailed to say

there will not be an extraordinary meeting of the board."

She said it in her usual calm manner, but he'd worked with her long enough to hear the vague question in her voice.

"Sir Malcolm," he replied succinctly and heard her sigh in understanding.

"Well, you can put that aside for now." Then she continued briskly. "All but three of the classic-car and rally clubs have submitted their routes and gimmick clues, and I've called the others, requesting they send them by the end of the week, no later. The last thing is…"

She went on talking, but the mention of Sir Malcolm diverted David's thoughts to the conversation he'd had with Val earlier. It was strange how easily she'd put things into perspective with just a few words and a gentle joke. Somehow, now, the older man seemed far less of a threat than David had previously thought, although nothing had really changed.

Except for those intimate moments when he'd opened up to Val.

Intimate moments.

Immediately his mind jumped to holding Val in his arms, her plump, soft breasts brushing his chest, her lips opening to his tongue, the sucking motion of her mouth, which caused his brain to short-circuit. He couldn't remember a time when he'd been so aroused, so quickly. Like her mouth held a quick-acting aphrodisiac that rushed through his veins, creating devastating heat and making him hard.

He'd wanted to pull her even closer, so close that only if they were naked could they get any nearer. Thought what it would be like to cup her buttocks and lift her, so she'd imagine how it would be if she were to open her legs to him, take him deep into her body.

Had she been as wet as he was hard? If he'd lifted her skirt and been able to get into her knickers, would she be hot and slick—ready for him, the way he'd been for her?

"So, which would you prefer, David?"

Rolly's voice broke him out of his erotic dream, finding him disoriented and indescribably turned on, which is the last thing he wanted his PA to know. He also hadn't heard a word she'd said, so in an effort to disguise that fact he replied, "You do what you think is best."

Shocked silence met that response. Then she said, "I'm sorry? What?"

Best to carry it forward with some kind of authority.

"Rolly, you make a decision, and let me know. You and I have worked together for more than five years, and there's no one I'd trust more than you to do the right thing."

She stuttered, and in her confusion he heard his own overwhelming need to constantly be in control of every little thing. Just the realization of how tightly he always held the reins was food for thought.

"If there's nothing else?" he asked, and he hung up when she hesitantly said no and goodbye.

When had he gotten that hidebound?

Oh, he'd always had the tendency to make sure everyone working with him knew he'd never ask them to do anything he wouldn't do himself, but that was different. Over the last decade he'd taken on more and more and delegated less and less.

Was that what Josh had been trying to point out to him when he'd asked if David planned to slow down?

And, even more importantly, why was he suddenly thinking about these things rather than concentrating on Rally Round and all his other responsibilities?

Even as the question crossed his mind, he knew.

"Damn, Valerie Sterling. I don't have time for you right now, and maybe I never will."

Yet, even as he said the words aloud, he heard the untruth in them and wondered what to do next. Because not doing anything probably wouldn't fly.

CHAPTER TEN

HAVING NO FURTHER appointments for the day, Val told Shala she was leaving early and went home, too confused and frazzled to give her best to her job just then.

On the bus ride home, she tried not to think about what had happened in her office, and the way she'd felt as she and David kissed. It had thrown her into erotic confusion, and now she wondered where the prosaic, no-nonsense woman she knew herself to be had disappeared to.

Once upon a time sex had been fun and something she craved. By the time her marriage ended, their love life had faded into drab routine, which Val rarely if ever initiated. She really hadn't missed Des when they broke up.

Thereafter, she'd been too exhausted by work, looking after the kids, checking on her mother, and doing housework to want anything more than to fall into bed and sleep. Over time, desire had waned into nothingness, and she'd stopped even wondering whether that was healthy or not.

It made no sense to stir a pot she had no interest in dipping into.

Yet, now there was no way to avoid the knowledge that with one kiss David had shattered the illusion of her being disinterested in the sensual side of life.

Val shivered, her body heating all the way through, as she chided herself for letting the memory rise again into her consciousness. But there was no way to stop it, really. It was indelibly ingrained into her mind, and there was no way to suppress it.

And how she'd behaved in response to that kiss!

He must have thought her a love-starved beast from the way she'd sucked his tongue into her mouth and pressed so close, as if to disappear into his body. Every atom inside had strained toward him, and if he'd taken her clothes off right there and then, she'd have done nothing to stop him.

In fact, she would have been an eager assistant, desperate to feel his hands—and anything else he wished to share—on her body.

That realization should be shocking, but Val couldn't bring herself to care. After all, what had happened that day probably wouldn't be repeated. Hadn't David said he didn't have time for her?

At least, in that respect, he was being completely honest, although that didn't stop his words from hurting.

And while he said it as though that were a temporary situation, she didn't believe it. Even before he'd conceived of Rally Round, Val had been aware of his presence in the transplant world and how his name seemed to crop up everywhere. If he wasn't guest-speaking at some conference or hospital, he was making the rounds of fundraisers. And that didn't include any of his consultancy work, which wouldn't receive the publicity the rest of his life did.

As she walked the short distance to her front door, she rather sourly considered how much easier it would be if David Kennedy were just a handsome, sexy man. If he'd continued to present himself in that initially cold, arrogant way, she could discount his appeal as not worth thinking about.

Instead, each encounter they'd had revealed different facets of his personality, each more intriguing and attractive than the last.

Letting herself into the house, she locked the door behind her before going down the narrow passage and into the sitting room. Out of habit, she turned on the TV, the low volume of sound giving the house some background noise, breaking the lonely silence.

Going into the kitchen, she put her handbag and tote on the counter before opening the fridge, trying to decide what to eat later but not really seeing anything she wanted. The transition from cooking for four, then three, then far too swiftly one, hadn't been easy. There were days when just the thought of fixing something for tea made her feel exhausted and she had to force herself to have a meal anyway.

On an afternoon like this, it was impossible not to wish there was someone else to share the rest of the day with, before retiring to bed. Funny to realize that until David had pulled her into his arms, she'd not missed having a warm, hard body beside her during the night, but now she was afraid she would.

"Okay, Valerie Denise Sterling," she said aloud, slamming the fridge door shut. She was channeling her mother by using her full name, just as Mum had when Val was in trouble. "That's more than enough of mooning over a man you hardly know when nothing will ever come of it."

Thoroughly annoyed with herself, she grabbed her bags and marched upstairs to her bedroom.

"A shower first, and then I'll think about food."

Stripping off her work clothes, she had a brisk shower. After toweling off, she realized she'd forgotten to bring her robe with her and padded, barefoot and naked, into her bedroom to get it. Passing the full-length mirror affixed to the wall, she paused and took stock of her body for the first time in years.

It wasn't too bad, she thought, turning first one way and then the other. She'd never been slender. Her breasts were ample, her hips wide, and her bum full, all a bit more than they had been when she was young. But while gravity was proving to be no friend, nothing was sagging horribly, and her active lifestyle kept her flexible and pretty well toned.

Yet, of course, she couldn't help noticing the imperfections—the silvery shadows of stretch marks, the wrinkles here and there, and…was that a gray hair in her pubes?

That warranted turning on a brighter light, so as to investigate.

Yes, damn it, it was a gray hair.

Who got a gray hair down there at forty-five?

Yet, why was she even worrying about that? She'd never been a looker. In fact, more than once in her younger days, compliments had been of the backhanded variety. She wasn't flashy at all. In fact, she'd been called *mousy* more than once, usually followed by placating comments about how nice her personality or character was.

But she was sure personality wouldn't be enough to make a man like David really interested. She'd seen lots of pictures of him with one gorgeous woman or another on his arm.

Not to say she didn't know her own worth as a woman. Her parents had raised her to be independent, to strive for the career she wanted, and to be the best she possibly could. If anyone asked, she'd admit to being proud of all she'd achieved in life, but she was also honest with herself about her shortcomings.

There was no way she could compete with those tall, model-thin, and mostly classically beautiful women David apparently favored.

And no number of kisses would ever change that.

Besides, who knew what the future held? The brief interlude earlier in the day might have temporarily taken her mind off the most pressing worries in her life, but there really was no escaping them.

Lifting her chin, she stared herself down in the mirror for a long moment, standing on first one leg then the other, flexing and clenching her fingers, before raising her arms above her head. Now her concentration wasn't on the extra girth around her waist or whether her breasts jiggled or swayed but on the sensation of her muscles—the still-fluid movement of her limbs.

Erotic excitement was all well and good but totally unnecessary. What was important was that her body hadn't begun to betray her—yet.

Deliberately turning away from the mirror, she walked over to her closet and, pulling out her terry-cloth robe, shrugged into it. Where before she'd been teetering between euphoria and shock, she was now back to normal, the sensible side of her nature reasserting itself, much to her relief.

Although there was also a twinge of sadness.

Forty-five wasn't old, as her sons seemed to think, but it certainly was middle-aged. She'd signed up to run in the rally because she wanted adventure, and she'd make sure to enjoy it because it might be all the fun she'd have for a long time.

She was about to grab her phone and head back down to the kitchen to find something to eat, when it rang.

Dr. David Kennedy

She froze, staring at the name on the screen, her heart immediately going into overdrive, her palms dampening and her knees getting shaky.

Answer or not?

But she was already reaching for it, even as the question entered her head.

"Hello?"

At least she was adult enough to keep her voice level, with just the right amount of question in it, to let him know she was surprised he was calling. That, despite the fact she had to sink down on the bed so she wouldn't end up in a puddle on the floor.

"I wanted to thank you again."

His words caught her by surprise.

"For what?"

"What you said earlier, about my mother. It has me thinking I've been sulking like a child when I should have let it go a long time ago."

He was using that laconic tone, but it didn't fool Val. Just the fact that he was speaking about his relationship with his mother told her all she needed to know.

"What do you plan to do about this new revelation?" she asked, glad he'd had a change of heart, but curious about whether he'd act on it or not.

He chuckled slightly before responding. "You're very task-oriented, aren't you? You see a problem and immediately set about making it right."

"I like to think I have a logical turn of mind, if that's what you mean." She knew she sounded defensive but couldn't stop herself. "What's the use of seeing something that's gone wrong and not at least making a plan to get it back on track?"

"I'm not complaining," he said quickly. "Believe me. Maybe if I'd had someone like you around before, things wouldn't have gotten this bad between Mum and me. I plan to call her this evening when I get home."

"Glad to hear it."

And she really was. Hearing David speak about the rift between himself and his mother had made her mostly sad, but there'd been a kernel of anger in her as well. When Mum died, the loss had been almost too much to bear. The sensation of abandonment, of becoming an orphan still lingered, even months later. While she could understand his anger at having never known his father, couldn't he see what a gift it was to still have his mother, alive and healthy?

Suddenly he said, "I should have asked before, but I hope I'm not calling at a bad time?"

"Not at all." All her concentration was fixed on their prior conversation, which was why she came out with "I just got out of the shower."

The silence on the other end of the line was telling, and Val closed her eyes in embarrassment, a blush firing up from her chest into her face.

"You do know that telling me you're naked while I'm driving down the M40 is a rather good way to get rid of me once and for all, right?"

"I didn't… I never…" Hearing herself blustering in the most ridiculous way, Val got the best grip on herself as she could and, after a deep breath, replied, "I never said I was naked."

"Are you?"

"No. I have on a robe!"

The sound he made had the hair all over her body rising, and her nipples peaked beneath the to figure out whether she'd done the right thing or not.

"I guess I'll know after this weekend," she muttered as her racing pulse finally began to slow.

How could twenty-four hours suddenly seem like a lifetime away?

onslaught of gooseflesh peppering her chest, back, and arms.

"With nothing underneath?"

It was a low, feral growl, and Val bit back the moan rising in her throat.

She should put a stop to the conversation right there and then. Demand he ring off if he'd said all he needed, but she didn't want to. What she wanted, instead, was to see how far it would go, irrespective of the fact that she would probably be left wanting more than she could have.

"Nothing," she confirmed, trying to sound matter-of-fact, although tremors were shivering over her skin.

There was that sound again—the one that turned the tremors into a shudder of desire run amok.

"Now I want to turn around and head back to Liverpool."

There was no amusement in his voice, just need so raw her own arousal grew in response.

"Why?" she asked, not to be coy but because she wanted to know whether he was feeling even a fraction of what she was. And to try to understand what it was about her that could possibly be causing him to want her so.

"Because I can still taste you on my lips, feel your body against mine. The scent of you is rising off my shirt to fill my head, and all I can think is that I want more. So much more."

"I don't understand why this is happening." It was little more than a whisper, but she knew he'd heard by his sharp intake of breath. "But I feel the same way."

"Does *why* matter?" he asked, still in that low tone, which vibrated through her bones and then out into her blood in a hot wave. "Can't we just enjoy the fact that it is happening and make the most of this unexpected gift?"

"Make the most of it?"

"Yes." There was a decisive note in his voice. "I don't know about you, but I couldn't tell you when last I've felt this way about anyone, and I want to explore it further. This kind of attraction doesn't come along every day, and I don't want to take the chance of walking away and then regretting it."

She knew what he meant. Didn't they have more life behind them than they could realistically expect to have ahead?

Yet, her main reason for turning down his dinner invitation before was still completely valid.

"I'm not prepared to have a relationship, with anyone," she told him. "And, as I said before, even if we have a fling, being seen with you will place me squarely in a spotlight I have no interest in."

The silence that followed had her holding her breath, although she wasn't sure why.

Then David said, "Come and stay with me this weekend—no strings attached. It'll give us a chance to figure out what we want to do in a private setting."

Tomorrow was Friday. Not much time to think. Should she go?

"But you must be run off your feet just now, with the rally a couple of weeks away."

It was an attempt to give herself more time to consider the possible ramifications, when inside she just wanted to agree without any further thought.

"Everything is pretty well in hand," he said. "And I'm confident the foundation staff can handle anything that comes up unexpectedly. If you don't want to drive to Oxfordshire, I'll come and pick you up in the afternoon, if you'd like."

"I'll drive," she said, surprising herself at how quickly the decision had been made. "Just text me the address."

"Wonderful." There was no mistaking the triumph in his tone, but Val couldn't bring herself to mind. "I'll send you the address and look forward to spending some time with you."

Then, before they could get into any more conversations about her state of undress, she ended the call. Sitting on the edge of her bed, Val tried

CHAPTER ELEVEN

WHEN DAVID SAID he lived in Oxfordshire, Val had assumed he was near the city of Oxford, renowned for its medical-research facilities. That would have made perfect sense, in light of his occupation and interests. But a look at the directions on her phone showed his home was further north and closer to Liverpool than she'd expected.

Afire with anticipation and a healthy dose of fear, she'd spent the afternoon after their call alternatively rifling through her wardrobe and trying to talk herself out of going.

She had, in her opinion, absolutely nothing worth wearing.

Even her nicest clothes and underwear were outdated and a little tatty.

When she realized she was contemplating the state of her unmentionables, she blushed and couldn't help giggling. Oh, David may have said it was a no-strings arrangement, but if the timing were right and they both wanted it, Val wouldn't object to getting intimate.

The urge to grab ahold of life with both hands, while those hands still worked the way they should, was driving her forward. This was, in the truest sense, living for and in the present: refusing to let the past stop her or fears of the future deter her from this unexpected journey.

Since it was still early evening, she ran out to a department store and bought a couple of new outfits, a nice pair of casual shoes, and some pretty underwear. Then, on the way home, she stopped at the neighborhood launderette and sanitized the new panties, suppressing chuckles the entire time.

She was, she knew, acting like a teenager planning her first sexual encounter but couldn't seem to control her excitement.

And why should she squelch it? Life really was too short to get caught up in the worry of what might happen. She'd go into this with her eyes open and no expectations other than a good time with a man who could set her blood ablaze with one heavy-lidded glance.

With her bag already packed, she was on her way right after work on Friday. Just before she got going, she texted David to let him know she was on her way then, putting on her favorite radio station, she started the three-hour drive.

Spring was in the air, and she was thankful the rain they'd been having over the last few weeks had seemed to clear up. While it was hard not to think about what lay ahead, she forced herself not to try to figure out exactly what would happen when she arrived but, instead, concentrate on her driving.

Following the directions on her phone, she passed through a lovely village and then turned onto a narrow lane. David had given her more specific instructions, and she slowed slightly as she passed a signpost, on the lookout for the entrance to his driveway.

Stone gateposts loomed ahead on her left, and she turned in hoping she was in the right place, since she didn't see a house or any other signs of civilization.

Up a long, well-maintained drive, set between paddocks and the occasional stand of trees, and then, just as she was wondering if she should turn around or stop and call David, a house came into view.

More than a house. A jewel box of a Georgian mansion, complete with columns on either side of the sweeping front steps, that had Val whispering to herself, "Oh, crikey!"

As she slowly drove along the driveway, which curved around a fountain in front of the house, the door opened, and David stepped out. Where just moments before she'd seriously considered not stopping—overawed by her surroundings— now her heart leaped, and she brought the car to a halt.

He looked completely different. Although surrounded by the splendor of house and gardens, he was casually dressed, his smile was welcoming, and he appeared more approachable somehow.

He came around and opened her door.

"You didn't have any problems finding the place, I hope?" he said as she got out of the car.

"No," she said, feeling suddenly almost shy, wondering how to best greet him, which made her voice take on a brisk, no-nonsense tone. "Your instructions were spot-on."

Then he bent and kissed her cheek, his lips lingering softly against her skin for a moment longer than strictly necessary, but not as long as she'd have liked.

"Thank you for coming."

He'd straightened slightly, but just enough that the contact between them was broken and the sensation of his breath across her cheek was sublime.

"Thank you for inviting me."

Such polite words, which Val knew had nothing to do with what either of them was feeling or really wanted to say. The temptation arose to turn her head enough to meet his mouth with hers, but she held back.

If she started kissing him now, outside of his house, she might not want to stop.

David apparently felt the same, as he pulled back far enough to meet her gaze with his own, and his expression had heat firing out from her chest to all her extremities.

"Come inside," he said. "Let me get your bag."

"Thank you."

But neither of them moved for a long moment, and Val's heart seemed destined to hammer its way right through her chest and fall at his feet.

David moved first, gently touching her cheek, where his lips had rested.

"When you look at me like that, all I want to do is toss you over my shoulder and run off with you. But I promised myself I'd take things slowly, so I'll let you walk inside under your own steam."

A huff of laughter escaped her tight throat, and she stepped back, putting enough distance between them so as not to drag him close.

"I appreciate your forbearance," she replied, although she really didn't. Being carried off, having not to think or make choices, sounded rather lovely just then.

He nodded, his lips tilting up into a little smile that melted her even more. Then he stepped around her to open the back door of her car and take out her bag.

"You look gorgeous," he said, as they walked toward the front door. "That color makes your skin glow."

"Thank you," she replied, smoothing the collar of her brilliantly pink blouse, the silky fabric a tactile treat. "I love it too. It's so bright and cheerful."

"That's my mother's signature color, so it's a favorite of mine," he replied, as he turned the massive ironwork handle and pushed open the thick oak front door.

"Is it?" Suddenly self-conscious, she could only hope he didn't think she'd worn it on purpose because of that fact. "I didn't know."

He slanted her an amused glance, his smile both teasing and reassuring.

"Cerise is her name, and she's certainly taken that to heart over the years, but unless you're a fan, you wouldn't have known. She was popular way before you were born."

They were in a massive, double-height vestibule, with tasteful black-and-white marble tiles and, at the other end, a sweeping central staircase leading to a landing on the floor above. High above them was a brilliant chandelier, and there were doors both to her right and left, all of them closed. Val couldn't help gaping at the splendor of it all.

"How beautiful." She turned to him, found his gaze fixed on her face, so that it took an effort to ask, "But it's so huge. How do you manage?"

"By closing off most of the rooms, and having a company come in twice a year to air everything out and give it a good clean. I only use a small part, or I'd be rattling around like a pea in a basin."

"That makes perfect sense."

"I'll show you around tomorrow, if you'd like. The rooms themselves are worth a look, although most of the furniture is under covers."

Before she could reply, a sharp yap came from the other end of the house, and David chuckled. Placing his hand gently on the small of her back, he led her toward a small door, recessed into the wall, to the left of the staircase.

"We've been summoned. Apparently His Highness has decided he's been ignored long enough."

"Oh, you have a dog?"

"A recent acquisition." The humor in his voice was evident. "I don't know what I was thinking at the time, but I've become attached anyway."

They were going along a narrow corridor, most likely once used by the servants. Almost at the end was another door, and David opened that to reveal a large room, obviously used as both living and dining rooms. And there, prancing about as though he hadn't seen his master in eons, was the dog that had jumped into David's lap during his TV interview.

"You adopted him," she cried, ridiculously wanting to cry but grinning instead.

His lips twitched into a rueful smile as he

scratched behind Gryphon's ear. "You saw Griff maul me, live on television?"

"I did." It was impossible not to laugh at his words and the ecstatic expression on the dog's face. "He's adorable."

As though realizing he was the topic of her conversation, Griff turned his attention to Val and came toward her, his tail going so hard it was a blur, and his bum wagged with it.

"Oh, you sweet thing," she crooned, enamored by his tongue-lolling smile and one-up-one-down ears. "Come and get some love."

Was it ridiculous to be envious of a dog? If it was, then David knew himself to be the height of absurdity, because he wanted to be the recipient of Val's every attention.

And yes, he'd even take it in the form of the belly rubs Griff was getting, if those were all that was on offer.

He'd been loitering in the vestibule for ages, waiting to hear her car approach, even though he had no idea when she'd actually arrive. Feeling like a randy teenager. Tempted to revert to childhood and start biting his nails again, although he'd stopped when he was about six.

Then, when he'd opened her door and she'd looked up at him with those gleaming, gemstone eyes, his heart had done a crazy flip. Gripping the door tight so as not to drag her straight into his arms, he'd been shocked at the visceral nature of his reaction.

There was something about this woman that called to him in a way no one else did. And not just physically, although his hands itched to touch and explore every inch of her body. Since meeting her, he'd mentally gone over every conversation they'd had, wanting to understand her and know her more intimately than he'd ever known any other.

With her, he felt he could be himself. Just plain David. Not Dr. Kennedy, or Cerise Kennedy's son, or even the inheritor of Sir Arthur Knutson's wealth.

Just a man, with thoughts and feelings he longed to share and felt he could confide to her.

She looked up just then, beaming with pleasure from her interaction with Griff, but whatever she saw in his expression had her smile faltering and her eyes darkening.

And, just like that, he knew once more—was reassured—that she felt it too. The electricity that flowed between them.

The desire.

Need.

He forced himself to smile and be casual as he said, "I prepared some supper. Would you like to rest a bit or eat now?"

"Whatever suits you," she replied, still stooping down to pet Griff.

"Now, then, I think," he said, in need of something to do with his hands. "It stays light late enough that I can show you the gardens afterward."

"Sounds wonderful."

"I'll just be in the kitchen," he told her and reluctantly tore himself away to put dinner together.

He'd set the table, and most of the food was ready. The lamb roast and potatoes were still hot, and all he needed to do was steam the fresh asparagus for a few minutes. While they were cooking, he took the garden salad to the table.

"There's a bathroom just through that door," he told Val, pointing her in the right direction as he went back for the rest of the food. "If you want to wash up."

Dinner was a success, with Val appreciative of his culinary skills.

"I taught my sons how to cook," she told him with a laugh. "But I have no idea whether they're any good or not. Clayton had no interest, and Liam did everything he could to get out of his turn, although I never let him get away with it. Each Sunday one or the other had to cook the evening meal, and no matter how bad it was, we all had to eat whatever they'd cooked."

"Are they both still at home with you?"

He thought he saw a flash of pain in her eyes, although she was still smiling.

"No. Clayton originally left to go to uni in London but decided it wasn't for him and started working as an apprentice with a bricklayer instead. He's doing well and still living in London, so I only get to see him every now and then. Liam..." She hesitated and then lifted her chin, as though to deny the words the chance to hurt. "Liam decided he wanted to go and live with his father about six months ago. Des—my ex—is in Newcastle, where we all used to live before the boys and I moved in with Mum, so it's a bit of a haul."

Although she was being deliberately casual, he could hear the hurt in her tone. He'd assumed that when she advised him to let the past go and rebuild his relationship with his mother, she was thinking about the pain of losing her mother. Now he realized, as a mother distanced from one of her sons, she was probably also sympathizing with Cerise.

"I'm not speaking out of school when I say the rally will be going through Newcastle, so maybe you can arrange to meet up with him while you're there."

Her eyes lit up, and then her lips turned down slightly as she said, "I'll mention it to him and see what he says."

The way her excitement peaked and then faded left him wondering what had happened between them, and he wanted her to know if she wanted to talk, he was more than willing to listen.

"Did you have a falling-out?"

"Not really," she said, then was quiet for so long that he thought that was all she was willing to say. Then she shrugged and continued. "After Mum died, and I got hired to work at St. Agnes, he decided he didn't want to move to Liverpool. Although he hadn't spent that much time with Des over the years, I guess he thought going somewhere familiar was better than a whole new city."

Still sensing there was more to the story, he was about to probe further, but she changed the subject to the provenance of the asparagus. Then they were talking about the farming activity taking place on his land.

"Sir Arthur bought this estate back in the sixties, when the original owners couldn't afford to keep it anymore. Luckily for me, in the long run, he was a financial and taxation genius. When he died, the death duties were minimized, and I was able to pay them and still retain the house without worrying about maintenance costs because the farmland is so productive."

Her eyes were wide, questioning, but then she looked down at her plate without saying whatever it was that was on her mind.

"I thought about giving it over to the National Trust," he continued when she remained silent.

"And even considered signing it over to his nieces and nephews, who claimed it was a part of their family legacy. But once they started making my life miserable, I decided to keep it, more out of spite than anything else. And here I am, fifteen years later, and I still haven't figured out what I ultimately want to do with it."

"You could leave it to your son."

He chuckled and shook his head. "Josh has already made it completely clear he isn't interested in inheriting it. Realistically, even though my mother moved in entertainment circles when I was growing up, the type of wealth I fell into is alien to both me and Josh. I never wanted or expected it, and it holds no great interest to him either, and I'm glad of that."

She chewed thoughtfully for a moment, and then, having swallowed, said, "It must have been so strange for you when it all happened."

Funny to realize her words brought him neither anger nor pain nor embarrassment. Since the entire debacle all those years ago, that had been his instinctive response when thinking about his father and the inheritance. Now, suddenly, those emotions were gone, and he searched to figure out why but could find no answers.

So instead, he just smiled at her and said, "It was a crazy time, but I've been able to move past it."

And the relief he experienced at the truth of

his statement created a sense of euphoria, which must have shown on his face, as Val's eyes widened slightly, and she smiled in return.

"If you're finished," he said, wanting to kiss her so badly his skin felt overheated and too tight, "we could go for a walk in the gardens."

"I'd like that," she replied, then chuckled as, at the same time, Griff jumped up from his bed and gave a low woof. "I guess he knows what W-A-L-K spells."

"He does, indeed. It's one of his favorite words. Although I think he's now learned T-R-E-A-T too, and that's his absolute favorite."

She laughed, her face alight with amusement, and David's breath caught in his chest at the sight.

Gathering his control, he said, "Come on, then. Let's get some fresh air."

Hopefully that would cool his ardor, at least a little bit.

CHAPTER TWELVE

AT THE REAR of the mansion, which David told her was called Guildcrest House, was an elegant marble terrace with wide steps leading down to a manicured lawn surrounded by flower beds.

"I can just imagine the parties they must have had here," she said. "All the ladies in beautiful dresses, the men resplendent in their evening clothes, standing around sipping cocktails."

She was trying to make small talk, to fend off the ever-quickening surges of attraction and desire urging her to move closer to him and touch him.

He'd said he wanted to take things slowly, but Val realized that wasn't what she wanted at all. If she'd been honest with herself, she'd have known that from the moment she'd run out and bought new knickers, but she hadn't wanted to admit it.

Now, strolling beside him in the evening glow of sunset, she couldn't help being fully, totally aware of his every movement, every breath. The sound of his voice was a caress to her senses.

The anticipation of getting close to him was an invitation to sin.

And she could hardly wait.

They strolled across the lawn toward a hedge, and Val's temperature rose as David took her hand in his. The conversation was still general—light and meandering from one inconsequential subject to the next—but the majority of her attention was on the feel of his fingers on hers.

There was a cleverly placed path between the tall shrubs of the hedge, offset so it was invisible until you were right beside it, and David led her through, into a secluded garden space.

"This is, I understand, called a knot garden," he said as he paused so she could appreciate the intricate design of the shrubs and flowers. "And my gardener informed me it was one of the finest in England, so it had to be preserved."

"It's gorgeous. I can see why he's adamant about it."

On they walked, Griff snuffling about and then running ahead, as though knowing where his master was going. On the far side of the garden, there was another opening in the surrounding hedge and, on going through, Val came to a halt with a gasp.

The house itself commanded far-reaching views, but from where they were standing the land sloped gently away to a lake with an island in the middle, creating a fairy-tale vista. The illusion was compounded by the humpback bridge crossing the water and the delicate gazebo at the center of the island, all gleaming in the setting sun.

"Oh, David. How lovely."

"I thought you'd like it," he said quietly. "Would you like to walk down to it?"

"Yes, please."

There was a terraced path and, as they sauntered down it, the light breeze picked up, making Val glad of her long sleeves. Griff had partially circled the lake and sniffed his way into the trees bordering the water, disappearing from view.

"Will he be okay, loose like that?" Val asked, worried, knowing David had only had the pup for a little while.

"Yes. There's actually a fence on the other side of the woods, to keep the farm animals out, so he can't go too far. Besides, I've brought him down here almost every evening, and he seems to realize I only spend about thirty minutes, so he always comes back before I'm ready to leave. If there's one thing Griff likes, it's his creature comforts. There's no way he's sleeping rough rather than in his comfy bed."

That made her chuckle, and she was still smiling as they crossed the bridge and she got her first real look at the gazebo. It was built like a very fancy summerhouse, with creamy stone floors and glass on all sides, some of the panes having sheer, flowing drapes. When David opened the door, Val saw there were upholstered couches and chairs, along with metal occasional tables and a selection of indoor plants completing the dreamy look.

David closed the door while Val walked across to look out over the water and the wooded landscape beyond. The moon was rising on the horizon, and they stood side by side watching the silvery disk slide into view, as evening faded to the first softness of night.

It was the most romantic setting Val had ever been in, and it would be perfect if David would stop being so damn noble and kiss her.

Or perhaps she should just take the bull by the horns instead?

Without giving herself time to develop cold feet, Val turned and found his gaze fixed on her face, and the temperature at her core rose, so she was assailed by the sensation of melting.

"I should like to make love here," she said, refusing to be shocked at her own boldness, although she could feel a blush heating her cheeks. "It's so beautiful, it's almost surreal."

"As are you," he said, in that low, rasping tone that never failed to excite.

She wanted to argue, to tell him she didn't need his pretty lies, but the way he was looking at her seemed to say that, to him, it was the truth.

Something bloomed inside her—a sense of

rightness, of being perfect, and in the perfect place, with the perfect man, at the perfect moment. It gave her the confidence she needed to make the first, desperately wanted move.

"Would you object if I kissed you?" she asked.

He didn't reply in words but in actions, opening his arms, stepping forward to meet her, as she aligned her body with his and raised her lips.

Once again David surprised her with his gentleness, although there was no mistaking the passion behind his kisses. He teased and tasted, luring her into a sweet erotic stupor with his mouth, until she was gasping, wanting more and more.

When she captured his tongue between her lips, she held onto a modicum of control, enough to take a lesson from his book. Slowly, softly she sucked, hearing him growl with pleasure as she teased him in return.

He raised his head fractionally. "Val…"

She heard the question in his voice and burrowed her hands beneath his shirt to touch his heated skin. "No. Don't stop," she said, rejoicing as goose bumps rose beneath her fingertips and his muscles rippled against her palms. "Don't you *dare* stop."

Then he was kissing her again but harder now, the command in his lips unmistakable. Slowly he eased her backward, holding her hostage with his plundering mouth, until her legs bumped one of the soft, upholstered seats. Then he eased her down to sit. Only then did his mouth ease away from hers to trail heated kisses to her ear.

"I want to see all of you. Touch all of you. Kiss every inch of your skin. Will you let me do that, Val? Will you let me make love with you in the moonlight?"

"Yes," she whispered, without an iota of hesitation. "Yes, *please*."

He knelt at her feet, as he had that day in her office, and she watched him slip first one of her shoes off, then the other. His fingers caressed her arches, then ankles, and she pressed her legs together, imagining those hands traveling up to her thighs and beyond.

But she was wearing trousers and cursed herself for it.

He rose and held out his hands to her. When she placed hers across his palms, he tugged her gently to her feet and turned them both so he could sit, keeping her standing in front of him. Then he unbuttoned her cuffs, before setting to work on the placket of her shirt. By the time he'd pulled the tails out of her waistband and undone all the pearly buttons down her front, she was shivering with reaction.

"Are you cold, sweetheart?" He held the two sides of her blouse closed across her chest, as though to keep her warm. "Would you prefer we go back to the house?"

"I'm burning up, David. Please, don't stop."

He groaned, the sound tipping another tremor along her spine, and slid the satiny fabric along and off her arms.

Holding her waist, he looked at her in the gloom, and his fingers tightened slightly on her skin.

"I feel as though I've waited for this moment forever," he growled. "And now that it's here, I'm almost afraid to move forward."

Oh, she understood that impulse all too well, but she had no intention of giving in to her fear.

"Do you want to stop?" she asked, her voice a rasp. "I don't."

"No." The word cracked, making her knees tremble. "I don't think I can stop, now. I want you too much."

"Do you want me to finish undressing myself?"

"No." Another emphatic denial, and it made her smile. "Turn around."

She did as he demanded, so she faced away from him, and the moonlit night lay in front of her, almost too glorious to be real. His fingers brushed her, finding and unhooking her bra, but rather than pushing the straps off her shoulders, he held her waist and laid his mouth against her back.

A gasp caught in her throat as his tongue swirled circles down her spine and then up again, until she was panting, fighting to draw sufficient breath into her body.

When his hands cupped her breasts, Val wobbled on her feet, knees even weaker, her thighs trembling with want. The dual sensations had her arching and flexing, soft sounds of rising desire issuing from her lips with each breath, the moon wavering before her passion-struck gaze.

Then he pulled her back a little more, so her thighs were fully between his, and she realized he was undoing her pants, and shudder after shudder started firing through her flesh. She helped him as best she could to get them and her undies over her hips, lifting her feet at his command, and stepping out of them both.

She was naked, and his hands skimmed over her body slowly, almost reverently, pushing her need so high she was a quaking mass of desire, almost unable to stand anymore.

As though realizing she was on the verge of collapse, David eased her down onto his lap. Spreading her thighs over his, he opened them so the cool air touched her in the most intimate way, making her groan again with longing.

"Watch the moonlight, sweetheart," he whispered, his lips against her shoulder, even hotter than her skin. His erection pressed against her lower back, thrillingly hard. "Let me make you come in the moonlight."

"Please." Her throat was dry from the desperate gulps of air she was drawing into her lungs. "Yes, please."

His hands skimmed up her inner thighs, and she tensed in anticipation. Yet, he refused to be rushed, even as she mewled and lifted her bottom in invitation.

"Hush, darling. Relax," he said against her neck as his fingers found her core, and he groaned in turn. "God, you're so wet and hot. I want to be inside you so badly right now."

"Then, do it," she said, goading him, wanting him the same way. "Don't make me wait."

"Not yet." He bit down gently on her neck, heightening the sensations bombarding her. "Let me…"

His voice faded into a growl as his fingers explored her further, one dipping deep into her body, sliding in, then almost back out before reversing course again. She arched to meet it, spreading her legs even wider, wantonly demanding more. David complied, adding a second finger, stretching her deliciously.

The pressure inside her built. Her hips rocked in time with his hand, as they found the perfect rhythm, but it wasn't enough.

Panting, desperate for the orgasm she could sense teasing just beyond her reach, Val strained toward it, but David growled into her ear once more, "Relax, darling. Relax."

She tried. Took a deep breath, willed her muscles to go as lax as she could.

He thumbed her clitoris, the unexpected stimulation catapulting her into the hardest orgasm of her life.

She cried out, the waves so sharp, so hard, she no longer saw moonlight but stars dancing behind her tightly clenched eyelids.

As the sensations waned, David murmured, gentling her, although his hands were still on her trembling flesh, keeping her arousal simmering. They stayed that way for a few long, drugged moments, as Val's breathing slowed, and her heart rate got back into within normal parameters.

David sighed and kissed her neck, his breath washing over her and raising fresh goose bumps in its wake.

"The only way this could be more perfect is if I could have watched you come." His fingers moved, and Val gasped, arousal immediately washing her anew. "Later, I will."

"I like the way you think," she said, caught between need and amusement.

"Mmm," he replied, his teeth scraping a line of sweet pain across her shoulder. "But now…"

Before she knew what he was going to do, his hands moved to her waist, and he was getting to his feet, lifting her at the same time. When he set her down on the couch, she thought he'd undress but, instead, he knelt in front of her, and ran his fingers lightly up her calves, to the inside of her thighs.

"I want to taste you." He said it simply—a straightforward request—yet the erotic kick it gave her had her nipples peaking, and her belly quivered. "Will you let me?"

Unsure if her voice would even work just then, she simply let her thighs fall open, and in the dim light she saw his lips curve, and the tip of his tongue touch the lower one. She groaned, unable to stop the sound, and his teeth flashed as his smile widened.

"Watch the moonlight, sweetheart," he said again, as his head dipped.

She sagged against the back of the couch in anticipation, knowing, without a doubt, he was about to take her to even higher heights of pleasure.

And he didn't disappoint.

CHAPTER THIRTEEN

THEY WOULD HAVE made love there, in the gazebo, if Griff hadn't come scratching at the door just as David was starting to disrobe. His curse of annoyance would have made her laugh if she hadn't felt the same way about the situation.

"Damn dog," he groused, pulling his shirt back on over his head, while Val started getting dressed. "If I didn't like him so much…"

Val laughed, knowing it was at best an idle threat.

"Griff has you wrapped around his furry paw, and it would be his little finger if he had one," she teased, having seen the way David had fussed over Griff's evening meal. "If you could, you'd have fed him the lamb and potatoes instead of that fancy doggy kibble."

He chuckled, turning her around to button her blouse.

"The ladies at the shelter made me promise not to feed him human food, no matter how hard

he begged. Otherwise, I'd have just set a place
for him."

They were still chuckling together as they went
back over the bridge, but Val couldn't help looking back at the gazebo and the moon hanging
higher now in the sky.

She'd never feel quite the same about moonlight from now on.

They meandered back toward the house, hand
in hand, and Val marveled at David's control.
He'd lavished her body with attention, brought
her to orgasm thrice without any relief of his
own, but you'd never know it from the way he
strolled along, as though in no hurry at all.

Val wanted to start running but quelled the
impulse.

"I can't wait to get you into my bed," he said
quietly, his thumb brushing over her fingers.
"Right now I'm savoring the anticipation, but I
was hanging on to control by a thread back there.
I'm glad Griff interrupted when he did, or I'd
have probably embarrassed myself."

And then she understood.

Back inside, he locked up the house and settled Griff into his crate. Picking up her bag from
where he'd left it earlier, he led her down another
corridor and up a steep flight of stairs. When he
opened a door in the passageway above, he entered ahead of her to turn on the light and then
stood back so she could walk past him.

The bedroom was huge, with intricate plaster molding on the ceiling and huge windows that no doubt would bathe it in light during the day. There was a large sleigh bed, a couple of dressers, a dressing table, and a large bookshelf in the room, but it still looked sparsely furnished.

Setting her bag down on the rack at the end of the bed, David turned to look at Val, and suddenly she had no more interest in the room.

All she could see was him.

"Where were we?" she asked, already toeing off her shoes and unbuttoning her blouse.

He didn't move, his gaze fixed on her, as she methodically removed each piece of clothing until she stood unselfconsciously naked in front of him. When he didn't move, she lifted her eyebrows at him and shook her head.

"So am I the only one to be without clothes right now?"

Then she held her breath as he began to disrobe, going much faster than she had, and by the time he was naked too, she was struck mute with awed desire.

He was perfect.

Delicious, with his dark flesh stretched over toned abs, broad shoulders, and thick thighs. Formally dressed in his bespoke suits, the absolute strength of him was somehow hidden, while naked it was on full, glorious display.

"If you look at me like that, you might end up

in a hostage situation, because I'll not want to let you leave."

She licked her lips, wanting to tell him she might not want to leave on Sunday anyway, but she kept the words to herself.

David moved toward her, and she stepped forward to meet him halfway. As his arms went around her and his mouth sought hers, she distantly wondered why being in his embrace felt like coming home, but the thought was lost under the onslaught of sensation.

They moved to the bed, still kissing, hands all over each other, learning contours and parameters, seeking out special places that elicited gasps and growls and sighs of pleasure. David touched her as though she were precious, looked at her as though she were the most gorgeous woman in the world, and Val drank it all in.

No matter how this ended, she would always consider this one of the best nights of her life.

Moonlight and laughter, desire and pleasure, all wrapped together to create something both erotically charged and infinitely precious.

Watching him pull a condom out of a drawer in the bedside table, knowing he was oh-so-ready, she tried to get him to hurry, but David ignored her attempts. Instead, he brought her to orgasm once more with his mouth, and she couldn't argue once she saw the intensity of his pleasure doing so.

As she came down off the high, he confirmed her thought by saying, "I could do that all night. Just hearing the sounds you make, feeling you come apart, makes me happy."

"I can't complain," she said, between gulps of much-needed air. "But now—"

She rolled him onto his back and straddled his thighs. When she palmed his erection, his hips jerked, and his face tightened.

"Val, I'm on the edge."

It was a warning. Stark, with a feral edge that tempted her to tease him some more. Would that tender man disappear then? And who, or what, would replace him?

She swiped her thumb softly over the tip of his penis, found it slick, and felt a pulse at the base. His lips drew back, his nipples tightened, and his hands gripped the sheet on either side of his hips.

No, she'd resist the temptation to test his control—this time—because, in truth, she wanted him inside her right now.

Releasing him, she grabbed the condom and tore it open.

David held out his hand, fingers beckoning.

"Give it to me. If you put it on me, I won't last a minute more."

Silently she handed it over, watched as he slid it on almost roughly. When he'd finished the task, she slid up his thighs and leaned forward, placing her hands on his stomach.

"Shall I drive?"

"Yes, please," he said, sounding as though his teeth were clenched.

Then she hesitated, unsure for the first time that evening. He must have seen something in her expression, because he immediately touched her thigh softly.

"What is it?" She shook her head, feeling silly, but he persisted. "Tell me. If you've changed your mind, just say it. We don't have to—"

"No. Of course I haven't changed my mind, David. It's just…"

"What?"

"I haven't had sex in so long, I'm worried it won't be any good for you."

He sat up in one fluid motion and pulled her into a hard embrace.

"Don't think that way." He murmured into her ear, his voice comforting, totally without judgment or amusement. "To hell with me. I just want it to be good for you."

She leaned back so as to see his face, and the warmth in his eyes gave her courage. She nodded, but he didn't let her go.

"How about I drive this time?" he said, using her own words, so there was no mistaking his meaning.

When she nodded again, he gently tipped her off his lap, supporting her weight until she was lying on the bed with him leaning over her.

"You tell me when you're ready, Val. We don't have to rush."

She touched his face, moved by his tenderness. "I am ready, just a little afraid. It's been years…"

"If you change your mind, no matter how far we've gone, promise me you'll tell me so I can stop."

"I will," she replied, although she wasn't sure she would.

Using one knee, he parted her thighs to kneel between them. She tensed, and he stroked a hand along her thigh, the other over her stomach.

"Relax, sweetheart."

She expected him to position himself for penetration, but instead he stroked through her folds with a gentle finger, finding her clitoris and circling it. Val squirmed and spread her legs a little wider, lifting her bottom up off the bed as he slipped two fingers into her and began to stroke.

"Yes," he murmured, as she felt the now, once again familiar pressure building inside. "That's it, sweetheart. Is that good?"

"David, please. I'm ready. Now."

And she was. What he was doing felt so good, but it wasn't enough anymore. She wanted to feel him inside her, filling her to the brim.

She reached for him, to urge him near.

His fingers retreated, and she lifted her head to watch as, still on his knees, he positioned himself and then pushed forward, stretching her little by little.

How could she have worried? It was sublime, an amazing sensation that fired out from her core to fill her entire body.

Now, to her, he was going too slowly. Taking too much care.

So she wrapped her legs around his hips and pulled him close. As close as possible, so he was buried in her as far as he could be.

Caught by surprise, David shuddered, his back arching.

Then he was moving, trying to go slowly, his teeth gritted and his lips drawn back, visual evidence of his fight for control. Catching his rhythm, she added her own beat—a counterpoint that changed the intensity of sensation, increasing her pleasure.

"I can't—" He growled it, the speed and power of his thrusts increasing.

Suddenly, without warning, he thrust once more then held absolutely still. Val thought it was over, and she didn't begrudge him the orgasm, although it was hard not to beg him to go on, since she was so close herself.

When his thumb found her clitoris, she cried out, lifting her hips, already barreling toward the cliff edge once more, going over in an instant.

And taking him with her.

* * *

David drifted up from sleep the following morning, then was rudely jolted wide awake when he realized the bed beside him was empty.

Had he dreamed the entire night with Val?

No. It had been real and one of the best of his life. They'd made love until early in the morning, their desire unquenchable, the passion between them unmistakable.

Only when, obviously exhausted, Val had fallen asleep in his arms, did David reach over and turn off the light. Lying beside her, savoring the sweet weight of her in his arms, he'd relived the evening in his head, committing each moment to memory all over again.

It felt right to have her here. Very few people got invited to Guildcrest House, and he'd never brought a lover back to his country retreat. If he was taking a woman home, it was to his London flat, at the top of the town house where the foundation was headquartered. He didn't consider that home. Not like Guildcrest, although it had taken him years to admit he actually liked the house.

Seeing it through Val's reactions had made it even more special, and he'd never look at the gazebo in quite the same way again. Just thinking about it now was making him hard all over again.

Which brought him back to the question: Where was Val?

Sitting up, he was relieved to see her bag was

still on the rack at the foot of the bed. At least he could be assured she hadn't taken off back to Liverpool. Just the thought made his teeth clench.

Getting out of bed, he went to the window and pulled back the curtains, and there she was, walking through the walled garden at the side of the house, Griff jauntily trotting beside her.

And, just like that, David felt the stress he didn't even realize had tightened his shoulders and neck dissipate.

Hurriedly washing and dressing, he made his way downstairs and into the kitchen, where he found a pot of tea, still hot, on the hob. Pouring himself a cup, he followed her outside.

It was quite early, the grass wet with dew that the weak morning sun hadn't had a chance to burn off yet. Going around the corner of the house to the garden gate, he watched Val go from flower bed to flower bed, touching a bloom here, bending to sniff another there.

Griff noticed him first and let out a happy bark as he ran over to David. Val looked up, and David couldn't help smiling at the little wave of pink that touched her cheeks, as he opened the gate and went through.

"Good morning," he called, still watching her even as he bent to pat Griff, who was capering around his legs. "Sleep well?"

"Like a log," she replied, with a sly twist of her lips. "You?"

"Never better."

The pink deepened on her cheeks, and she looked away, waving her hand at the open space left in the center of the garden.

"This would be a great place for a vegetable patch. How come you haven't put one in?"

He shrugged. "I'm not much of a gardener, and the tenants are happy to sell me produce. Besides, I'm not here consistently enough to make it worthwhile."

She frowned slightly and looked around once more. "That's a shame. It's south-facing, so it would be perfect for it."

Then she seemed to shrug the thought off, as she moved toward him, and he stepped forward to meet her halfway, bending to place a firm, lingering kiss on her delectable mouth. Her lips were a little puffy, and he felt no guilt knowing it was his attentions that had given them that bee-stung pout.

In fact, it gave him great pleasure.

"Thank you for the tea," he said, wondering if it would be overdoing it to suggest she come back to bed. "Would you like some breakfast?"

"Thank you. That would be lovely."

How polite they sounded. It was so British, he had to chuckle.

"What's so amusing?" she asked, slanting him a questioning glance, as they walked back to the house.

"We are," he replied. "And it reminds me of my mother saying you could run over an Englishman with your car and, while he was being taken to the ambulance, he'd apologize for having gotten in your way."

He opened the door for her to precede him into the house, and she paused on the threshold to look up at him.

"So which of us got run over last night?"

"I'd say me," he admitted. "And if you give me a moment, I'll find your car keys so you can do it again."

She laughed and walked farther into the room to stand beside the kitchen table, putting her mug down on it.

"I'll be happy to be of service," she said, her eyes darkening, and the corners of her lips twitching into a sultry smile. "In fact, there was something I wanted to do last night but never got around to. I'm out of practice, but hopefully it'll come back to me with time."

That look in her eyes, the way she bit her lower lip, had his pulse pounding in an instant.

"Oh?" He was almost afraid to ask what she meant but didn't have to, as she took his hand and led him into the living room, firmly closing the kitchen door so Griff couldn't follow them.

And it was a long time later before they had breakfast, but their appetites were extremely good, whetted by vigorous and satiating lovemaking.

CHAPTER FOURTEEN

For Val, the weekend was revelatory and went by all too quickly. Having been convinced there was little in life left to look forward to, she now had to admit her bleak outlook may have been a bit pessimistic.

Make hay while the sun shines was an expression her mother had been very fond of, and Val was beginning to appreciate the advice.

They'd made love—a lot—and talked about their lives, which had made her even more aware of how boring her existence had been in comparison to his.

David had grown up moving from one grand location to another with his mother and been surrounded by her fabulous and famous friends. The list of singers, costume designers, entertainers, and actors he'd met as a child, some of whom he referred to as *Uncle* or *Aunt* was impressive. But one of the important things she'd learned during their time together was the origin of the stiff, cool persona he used as a shield.

"My mother's way of dealing with celebrity hounds was to constantly smile and seem full of joy and friendliness while never actually allowing anyone she wasn't sure of to get close. I found it easier to assume a standoffish persona, and the practice I got into in childhood served me well later on."

He didn't need to elaborate. That more recent part of his past was one she already knew.

Instead, she asked, "Speaking of your mother, did you call her, the way you said you wanted to?"

He gave a rueful smile. "I tried, only to find out she was cruising the Mediterranean on someone or other's yacht and won't be back to shore until next week. Trust Mum to be out of contact exactly when I want to speak to her."

Val smiled with him, glad to hear only gentle amusement in his voice.

By the time Sunday came, Val had to give herself a stern talking-to so as not to feel depressed about leaving. It was, after all, just a brief interlude—for them both.

"I forgot to tell you," David said, as he was walking her to her car before her departure. "The producer wants to interview Tamika for the documentary and suggested using a clip from it as part of the prerally promotion, which will be airing through a variety of news outlets."

Val smiled, as he put her bag on the back seat and closed the door.

"Tamika will like that. Let me know what the plan is, when you know."

"I will. They were suggesting they do the interview at the hospital, but that's up to your CEO and her parents."

Standing by her door, she nodded, wondering if they were talking about Tamika and the rally so as to avoid other subjects, like whether this was the last time they'd be together this way.

As though reading her thoughts, David said, "I'd like to see you again. Will you come and visit again next weekend?"

She wanted to say yes right away but hesitated, eventually saying, "I'm not sure I'll be able to. I'll let you know."

"Okay," he said, with a little smile. "Drive safely, and please let me know when you get home?"

"I will," she replied, stupidly warmed by his concern.

Then he moved in close and kissed her until her head swam and she clung to him for dear life. And they might have stayed that way until Monday morning if Griff, apparently feeling he was missing out on something important, hadn't jumped up on them.

"Not fair," she gasped as they broke apart and David got Griff settled down.

He just gave her a cheeky look from beneath those long, dark lashes and grinned.

But although he was smiling, his voice was serious when he said, "I can't get enough of you."

Before she could do something silly, like drag him back inside, she got into her car and started it. Then, with one last wave, she was on her way.

Every day that week at work dragged, with Val eager to get home in the evening, knowing David would call. She could hear his tension building, as Rally Round's start date came ever closer, and found herself encouraging him to talk about it, hoping to alleviate some of his stress.

Then, on Wednesday night, he told her he'd be in Liverpool that Friday, to participate in the taping of Tamika's interview.

"It's not scheduled until midafternoon," he said. "So I'm planning to take the train from London about midday and stay over that night, leaving Saturday morning."

"You could come and stay with me," she found herself blurting, having not given it even an instant of thought.

"I would love to." His voice dropped low, striking sparks in her belly and raising goose bumps on her back and arms. "I was hoping you would offer."

Not as good as spending the entire weekend together, but she craved his company and his touch too much not to grab what she could get.

Especially knowing whatever there was between them couldn't last.

Not that she'd want it to, anyway, she reminded herself stoutly. Although she'd be the first to admit she was totally smitten by him and completely overwhelmed by his lovemaking, they were chalk and cheese. With her being a stick of schoolroom chalk and David some kind of exotic, expensive cheese, like that one she'd read about made from Balkan donkey milk.

Just the night before, he'd told her about an upcoming gala event at the Theatre Royal, where even royalty would be present. He'd spoken about it as a nuisance that he had to attend on behalf of the foundation, while she'd been wondering who he'd take with him, both jealous and glad it wouldn't be her.

There was no way she'd fit into that type of lifestyle, even if she wanted to—which she didn't!

Besides, she reiterated to herself, at this stage of her life she had to be realistic. Giving her all to or becoming dependent on someone else wasn't what she planned to do ever again. If she'd learned anything over the years, it was to take care of herself and not expect anything of substance from others.

That way when they let you down or abandoned you, it didn't hurt that much, if at all.

David knew full well he was using the interview with Tamika Watkiss as an excuse to see Val again, and even though this wasn't the time to be rushing off out of London, he didn't care.

The memories of their time together had haunted him, and although he tried to give his all to his work, just as he always did, Val never truly left his mind. Often it felt as though he was living for their nightly calls, and although he realized their relationship couldn't develop the way he suspected he'd eventually want it to, he couldn't stay away. Or stop wanting her.

His life was devoted to GDK and always would be, and that devotion included a lifestyle Val had no interest in but David felt he needed to maintain, for the good of the foundation. Being absent most of the time, traveling about to keep things ticking over and to fulfill his roles as both CEO and consultant meant he was away from home more than he was in residence. No woman would stand for that.

He'd even been questioning his decision to adopt Griff, although God knew having that mischievous pup around had certainly lifted his spirits. But the way his ears drooped each time David left him behind—either with his housekeeper or

Rolly, both of whom doted on him and treated him like a prince—was a wrench.

Griff was a master at canine manipulation and guilt-tripping. David didn't need a woman getting in on the act and making him feel even worse.

He texted Val when he got to Lime Street Station, letting her know he had arrived. The interview was going to be at the Watkiss house rather than the hospital, and he was going straight there. As important as the interview was, David couldn't help just wanting it to be over, so he could see Val.

Tamika looked wan, and her eyes were sunken, but her spirits were high.

"I got my hair done," she told David proudly, showing off her braids. "And Mum got me a new outfit too." She lowered her voice and gave him one of her mischievous grins. "Mum had an awful row with Dad when she told him he had to wear a suit and tie, and he put his foot down. 'Let Dr. Kennedy wear a damn suit. I ain't wearing one.'" She giggled. "So don't be surprised if Mum tells you how nice you look, just to get a dig in at Dad."

It took everything he had to keep a straight face when, after greeting him, the very next thing Mrs. Watkiss said was, "My, don't you look smart in your suit!" and he heard Tamika's muffled laughter.

The interview went well. David had made sure

the interviewer knew Tamika wasn't to be tired, and they were to keep her part of the taping short. The teenager was wonderful—natural in front of the camera, forthright about her condition and her prospects too.

"I know I probably won't get the donations I need," she said, looking straight into the camera. "As Dr. David said, I'm in a minority and can't get a pancreas from a living donor. Not that many people sign up to be organ donors when they die, so that narrows my chances even more. But there are lots of patients who need organs they can get from live donors, and they might have a much better chance if donors sign up and get tested to see if they're a match."

After they'd filmed Tamika's part, they taped extra footage with her parents and older brother, as well as David, although he thought people were probably tired of seeing his face on TV.

Finally, it was over, and he texted Val, who texted him back a few minutes later to say she was on her way home and he could come over whenever he liked.

Instead of using a car service, he'd opted to rent a vehicle, so it was only a matter of putting her address into the navigation system and he was on his way. Ridiculous to feel his stomach twist and dip, as he drew closer to her house, and for his heart to be racing by the time he found a parking spot on the street.

Walking up the short driveway, it struck him how much her house reminded him of the one he and Georgie had bought when they'd first been married. Then the door opened, and all thoughts fled at the sight of Val's smiling face.

He made it inside before he dropped his bag on the floor and, as soon as she'd closed and locked the door, dragged her into his arms for a series of long passionate kisses. When they finally came up for air, he tried to convince himself to behave, but having her resting so pliantly against him didn't help.

"Hello," he said, his throat tight. "I guess I should have said that first, before mauling you."

She giggled and kissed the corner of his mouth so quickly he didn't have a chance to capture her lips again.

"I don't mind. And I'd say *Carry on*, except I have a pot on the stove, and I'd hate to burn dinner."

He followed her into the neat living room and then stood in the archway leading to the galley kitchen to watch her bustle around.

"That smells delicious."

"It's chicken paprikash. My mum's quick and easy version. It was our family's favorite meal when we were late getting home."

"We could have ordered in, to save you the effort."

She slanted him a look he didn't know how to interpret.

"I don't mind. Cooking is one of the few household chores I actually like. How did the interview go?"

"Perfectly, I thought. Tamika was a star."

He told her all about it, including about Mrs. Watkiss and the suit, which sent her into peals of laughter, which set him off too.

"And, because of that little wretch Tamika, I had to stand there, biting the inside of my cheek not to laugh out loud, while she's giggling away in the background. I couldn't look at either Tamika or her father in case they got me going."

"I'm glad I wasn't there." Val was doubled over, holding her side, still laughing, her eyes filled with tears. "Oh, I wouldn't have been able to restrain myself."

Just seeing her that way made his heart sing, although he tried to ignore the sensation.

Over dinner she asked about another patient he'd talked about, who needed a bone-marrow transplant but was proving impossible to match.

"Still nothing," he said, frowning, that horrid and all too well-known feeling of impotence flooding him. "We're running out of time for him, I'm afraid, although I'm hoping maybe with the help of the Rally Round campaign, there might be a miracle."

Then, because he hated that sense of having

his hands tied, he changed the subject to something less depressing.

After they'd finished eating, he helped her wash up, and as she dried her hands on a kitchen towel, she gave him a level look and said, "May I take you upstairs and have my wicked way with you now? I feel I've exerted as much restraint as should be reasonably expected of me."

"I thought you'd never ask."

They showered together, and David found it almost unbearably erotic. Val naked, wet and slick, was a complete turn-on. By the time they'd washed each other off, they were both panting, and he was tempted to pick her up and make love to her right there.

"Don't even think about it, David," she said, her voice firm, if tremulous. "Neither of us is as young as we used to be, and we know better."

So he laughed and stepped out of the shower, pulling her along with him.

"You're the boss," he told her, grabbing the towels off the hooks and leading her into her bedroom. "I don't mind either way, as long as you pay the toll for putting me off."

And he set about exacting sweet, passionate revenge, with nary a complaint from Val.

CHAPTER FIFTEEN

DAVID'S FAR TOO brief overnight stay was both extreme pleasure and, after he'd left to go back to London, way too much pain for Val's peace of mind. Physically she was sated, but emotionally she felt raw, while confusion clouded her thoughts. The quagmire of conflicting feelings left her restless, and she decided to take advantage of the sunny day to wash her car, just to get out of the house.

As she changed into suitable clothes, collected all the paraphernalia she needed, and went outside, her brain was still trying to process all that had happened the evening before.

Strangely enough, the things that stood out, causing her disquiet, had nothing to do with David's lovemaking, although she had to admit it could easily become addictive. No, the things that were stuck in her mind were actually simpler.

The first was the laughter they shared whenever they were together or even spoke on the phone. Not that Val thought of herself as taciturn or particularly ill-humored, but she hadn't laughed as much in years as she had over the last week. That shouldn't be a bad thing, but it did leave her questioning the path her life was on. When she eventually stopped seeing David, would she regress to that woman who barely smiled, who had no one to laugh wholeheartedly with?

Just the thought of it made her sad.

The second incident that kept circling her brain had occurred after they'd made love and were tangled up together under the sheets.

She didn't know where the impulse came from, but she'd come right out and asked him a question that had been on her mind since they'd first met.

"Why did you give up surgery? From all accounts, you were brilliant at it."

There'd been a part of her that wished he'd say it was because he'd inherited his father's billions and didn't have to work as hard anymore. It was what all the media outlets assumed to be the case, and if it were true, she knew he'd drop in her estimation, even with the foundation and whatever else he did.

He was silent for so long she wondered if he would even answer, and then he said, "Guildcrest House and his money weren't all I inherited from Arthur Knutson. I have palmar fibromatosis. Dupuytren's contracture."

Lifting up onto her elbow, she'd searched his

face. Nothing about his expression indicated any undue distress about it, but his eyelids were lowered, hiding whatever might be revealed in his eyes.

She knew what it was, of course—a thickening of tissue under the skin of the hand that, if untreated, could cause the fingers to bend permanently in toward the palm.

"But it usually happens to men over fifty and comes on gradually. You couldn't have been more than—"

"Thirty-four when I realized something was wrong."

He hadn't retreated behind his cool wall, but somehow this easy disclosure was worse, and she wasn't sure why.

"Once I found out, I stopped operating and sought treatment. Luckily, I was able to get into an experimental blind study, and it worked, although I was warned it might not be a cure, since at the time there was no way to be sure. I couldn't take the chance on it being a temporary fix. Not when peoples' lives would be at stake."

"And then you inherited the money."

"Actually, the two things—finding out about the Dupuytren's and about my father—happened almost simultaneously. And I later found out Arthur Knutson had the disease too, with early and severe onset, and obviously passed the gene for it on to me. Do you know what they used to call Arthur in financial circles? The Nordic Raider, in honor of his Scandinavian heritage."

"Viking disease," she'd murmured under her breath, suddenly remembering one of Dupuytren's other names.

"Mm-hmm."

Here was another secret David had shared with her. One that hadn't come out in the suit against him filed by his cousins or in any of the tabloids since. Many of the reports she'd read stated the *brilliant* surgeon, Dr. Kennedy, had abandoned his fast-rising career once he hadn't had to work for a living.

There'd been a sneering tone, as though high-minded people should condemn him for making that choice, the reports casting him into a greedy, grasping light.

As if anyone else, no matter what their profession, might not be tempted to give it all up if they were handed billions of pounds!

She couldn't help wondering, though, if there had been an inciting incident that caused him to seek treatment. After all, Dupuytren's really didn't come on swiftly, although, as he'd explained, his father had suffered from it too.

And, most importantly, why had he shared all of this with her?

Was it an indication of how much he trusted her or that he needed someone to confide in and she was handy? Or perhaps an amalgamation of both scenarios? Perhaps he thought she should feel honored to be entrusted with his secrets, but she truly didn't feel that way at all.

Instead, it felt like a burden.

By telling her information not in the public sphere, he was putting her in a position to do him harm, even inadvertently. So now it was even more imperative they keep their affair secret so she wouldn't accidentally let something injurious to him slip.

Another worry to add to her growing list.

This morning, before he left, she'd said, "This time next week, Rally Round will be underway. Are you ready for it?"

"As ready as I'll ever be," he'd replied, looking dapper in his suit and totally out of place at her small dining table. "Are you and Emma?"

"I think so. All except for making a final decision about the costumes."

He'd leaned back, eyebrows raised in question. "Costumes?"

She'd chuckled, saying, "Emma decided we're to wear 1960s outfits to go with her car, so she's been scouring secondhand stores for some. She didn't realize that most of the vintage styles—the ones that have stood the test of time, anyway—weren't made for a figure like mine. We're to meet up again later, so I can try on some of the new ones she's found."

His eyelids had drooped in that sexy way, and

he'd said, "Your figure is perfection, so the designers were the crazy ones. I can't wait to see what you come up with. And I have to say I'm jealous. I wonder if Josh would be willing to do something similar?"

"Top hats and canes, to go with the Daimler?"

"Something like that. And we can provide contrast for each other—the thirties and the sixties, side-by-side."

It was then she knew she had to make it clear that they couldn't be seen together during the rally. But when she'd said it, as though reminding him of a fact they both already knew, he'd retreated behind that laconic drawl as he'd agreed. And it felt as though their parting kiss was a cool, perhaps even final, farewell.

If that were the case, perhaps it was for the best.

She knew what she felt for him went beyond liking or physical attraction, and she couldn't afford to allow those emotions to grow.

Realizing she'd been standing in one place staring into space, she pulled herself together and went to fetch the bucket she'd filled with soapy water.

Enough woolgathering for one day. Yet, even as she started on her chore, thoughts of David kept intruding.

He was so focused, so completely dedicated to the foundation and its work. Turning what must have been a horrible time of his life into something worthwhile was inspiring. No matter how things ended with them—and they must end, if they hadn't already—Val knew she'd always treasure the memories of their time together.

She just had to make sure she didn't get used to having him in her life, since there really was no place for her in his, irrespective of how casual they kept their relationship.

That thought made her frown as she stretched to get at the very middle of her car's roof. But, as painful as the reality was, she wasn't taking the chance of losing sight of it either.

Val turned to rinse off her sponge, and the next thing she knew, she was falling and then hitting the wet pavement, hard.

Winded, she lay there, trying not to let the fear overcome her, and heard someone shout her name.

Damn it.

It was Tony, her new neighbor with the puppy-dog eyes, and he dropped to his knees beside her.

"Are you all right? Do you need an ambulance?"

"No," she said, batting away his hands, as he seemed set to try and pull her to her feet. "I'm okay. I just need a moment."

"You fell hard." He sounded as though he were about to panic, and Val's annoyance level rose with his words. "Are you sure you don't need an ambulance?"

"Tony," she said firmly, just two shades away from rudely. "Just stop, please. I need to self-assess, but I'm sure I don't need an ambulance."

He rocked back, giving her a hurt, hangdog look. "I'm just trying to help."

Ignoring him, she checked each extremity and joint, one by one, finding them all okay, although she was sure she'd have some bruises. She really had gone down hard, smacking her shoulder and hip on the cement.

Sitting up, she made one more check of her various parts, then rolled to her knees and got up without assistance.

"See?" she said to her neighbor. "I'm perfectly fine."

He looked slightly annoyed at being dismissed, his pleading gaze turning cold.

"Shame that fancy friend of yours didn't stay to help you, isn't it?"

She wanted to snap at him, held the impulse at bay by the skin of her teeth.

"I'm perfectly capable of washing my own car. So, excuse me while I get on with it."

And as he skulked off back to his side of the fence, she wasn't sure what scared her more—the thought of him having seen David leaving her house and possibly recognizing him or not knowing, again, what had made her fall.

* * *

He should be pleased. Happy, even.

Rally Round was on track to be a great success.

The board of directors—especially Malcolm—had been quiet, and there'd been no further interference with his plans so far.

His work commitments were under control.

He even had what was, for him, a somewhat regular sex life—something that had been sorely lacking for years—with a beautiful woman who made no demands on his time.

A woman with whom he could be completely and simply himself, without barriers or even secrets.

Someone he'd grown to trust implicitly but didn't have to commit to in any way.

Yet, there was a feeling of discontent gnawing at David's insides, and he couldn't put his finger on what it was.

On the train ride back to London from Liverpool, while he tried to concentrate on work, his brain kept drawing him to whatever that sore spot in his psyche was.

Poking at it, the way you sometimes can't help picking at a scab, even though it hurts and you know it won't do you any good.

Might, indeed, do harm.

David stared out the window at the scenery flashing past and tried to pinpoint the source of his dissatisfaction, but to no avail. Letting his mind roam, there were flashes of thoughts, none of which seemed connected.

Josh asking him when he would slow down.

The sensation of homecoming as he walked up to Val's front door, which reminded him of a simpler time, long past, as well as seeming to offer him something valuable in the present.

Rolly's surprise when he'd said she could deal with a problem herself rather than wait for his direction, and then again, when he'd told her he'd be taking last weekend off.

His mother's voice, Southern US accent now firmly overlaid with an upper-crust English one, as she'd followed his lead and told him about her Mediterranean cruise.

Mum had never been one to express too much surprise over anything, but he'd heard the questioning note in her voice, as he'd engaged her in the kind of chitchat that had been lost between them for years.

Just catching up, rather than a call about a specific topic or with an aim in mind.

At the end, she'd said, "You sound well, Davie. And it's been lovely hearing from you."

"It's been lovely talking to you too, Mum." And it had been. He'd never acknowledged it before, but missing her had left a huge hole in his life. "When will you be back in England? I'd love to see you."

"I didn't have any plans to go back, but... I could make some?"

Strange to hear Mum even slightly hesitant, but once he'd expressed the wish that she would, she became once more her bubbly, outrageous self, and he'd been grinning when he hung up.

Healing the rift between them had been long overdue. He'd decided not to ask any more questions about her relationship with his father or why she'd kept it all secret all those years. Realistically, it was of no importance. Knowing wouldn't give him back anything of what he'd lost or repair the parts of his heart that had been damaged, but forgiveness and understanding toward his mother definitely could.

Besides, as a parent himself, especially one who'd had a sometimes-rocky relationship with his son, shouldn't he have been more understanding all these years?

So he had work he loved and that kept him busy. He was mending the relationship with his mother and doing his best to nurture the one with his son. He had a... What could he call Val, really? She seemed to defy description. Lover, yes. But also a friend, he thought, and a confidante who both simplified and complicated his life.

Talking to her about the Dupuytren's contracture had been easier than he'd expected. The only people who knew about it before had been Josh, Mum, and David's doctors. It was something he'd never even wanted to speak about to anyone else. The urge had been there to even tell her about the worst bit—the episode that had kept him awake night after night for years, but he couldn't bring himself to do it. If he'd seen the same contempt in her eyes that he'd felt for himself, he wasn't sure how he'd react, but that would definitely have been the death knell of their relationship.

And although she'd made it clear that their relationship was only transient due to her need to stay out of the limelight and, realistically, his life generally, he didn't want it to end that way.

She'd reiterated the fleeting nature of their friendship again this morning, when she'd said they wouldn't be able to spend time together during the rally since they'd all be under scrutiny. What if they were caught together on the documentary crews' cameras?

He wouldn't care, but it was obvious she would, and that meant abiding by her decisions, which should be fine with him, shouldn't it?

Without having to think about Val or try to coordinate how they could meet up, he could put his full focus where it really needed to be, which was on Rally Round. After all, its success or failure could be make-or-break for the foundation and particularly his place in it.

And without GDK, he'd have next to nothing.

Why did that thought, which wasn't at all new, make him even more ill-tempered than before?

It was the way things had been for the last fifteen years and hopefully would be for another fifteen. He had Josh, the foundation, his renewed relationship with his mother, and he didn't need anything more.

Did he?

CHAPTER SIXTEEN

THE ATMOSPHERE AT the convention center in Edinburgh on the morning of the first day of the rally was electric. Crowds of drivers, navigators, onlookers, and well-wishers milled around, waiting for the start of the event.

Val tugged at the back of the A-line color-blocked mini she was wearing.

"Stop," Emma laughed, swatting at her hand. "It's not coming down any farther, no matter how you pull at it. Besides, you look fab. Your legs are terrific."

"Thank you for that. However, I feel ridiculous. How did I let you talk me into this, again?"

Emma just laughed and leaned against the fender of her bright red Mini.

"Thank goodness we're not too far back," she said. "Number fifteen puts us right about in the middle of the pack, and George and Tess are just ahead," she continued, referring to the friendly older couple they'd met the night before.

"Yes," Val agreed. "The middle of the group is a good spot to be."

She'd been surprised at the number of cars that had signed up for the rally, and the foundation had had to put a cap on it of forty. However, a lot of classic-car owners who hadn't been able to sign on had been encouraged to bring their cars out anyway and display them for the public. David had told her he hoped it would encourage even more people to come out and see the vehicles and hopefully sign up as donors or give blood at the same time.

Val looked around, realized she was searching the crowd for David, and couldn't get herself to stop. To one side the celebrity drivers, news anchor Ryan Winterhauer and comedian and documentary presenter Kaitlin Proctor, were holding court beside their Rover P4, signing autographs and posing for pictures.

Val and Emma had been briefly introduced to them the night before at the drivers' meeting, since the producers were running around, trying to line up times for interviews. It had been decided that on the leg out of Newcastle upon Tyne, Val would navigate for Kaitlin and be interviewed, while Ryan would navigate for Emma.

"Lovely to meet you," Kaitlin had said, her sharp blue eyes darting about the room, giving the impression she was looking for something or someone, her dangly earrings twinkling in the lights. "I'm sure we'll have a grand time."

When she'd strolled away, long, thin legs eating up the ground, her bum swinging like a church bell, and headed straight for David, Val had her answer. And when his dark head had dipped to hers and Kaitlin ran one of her earrings through her fingers, the rush of jealousy had taken Val by surprise.

And she'd despised herself for it.

David had been in full-on Dr. Kennedy mode: cool, calm, and collected man-about-town. Looking at him, it had been hard to reconcile that image with the intensely passionate man who'd knelt between her thighs in the moonlit gazebo and made her cry out in pleasure.

As though hearing her thoughts, he'd looked right at her, and Val had had to turn away so he wouldn't see the blush staining her cheeks.

Despite her thinking she wouldn't hear from him again, he'd called almost every night since the Saturday before. And although each time she hung up she told herself it was time to call a halt to their relationship, she'd somehow never got around to telling David.

Which was entirely unlike her usual straightforward approach to life.

Somehow she'd convinced herself they could carry on a little bit longer—that the twin specters of someone finding out about them and her having MS weren't yet urgent.

"Are you all right?" Emma asked, startling Val out of her musings.

"Of course. Why do you ask?"

"You were rubbing your arm and clenching and unclenching your fingers. Did you hurt yourself?"

She hadn't even been aware of doing it, and a cold stab of fear went through her stomach. But somehow, she was able to smile in the face of Emma's probing look and her own fear to say, "Oh, I took a fall last weekend, and I've been a little sore."

Thankfully, just then, there was a stir, and the crowd nearest to the building started to clap and then laugh. Val saw why, when David and a blond, younger man she recognized as his son Josh stepped up onto the stage. They were both dressed in full eveningwear, but from a bygone era, complete with top hats, satin capes, and canes. They were even carrying champagne glasses in their hands.

Then she saw Griff and sputtered with laughter. He too was wearing a cape and white tie. The only thing missing was the hat, which probably wouldn't have stayed on anyway.

"Ooh, those sneaks," Emma muttered. "I'd begun to think we were the only ones dressing up, but they've definitely stolen our thunder.

Even the dog looks like a swell from one of those black-and-white musicals."

"I wonder if he'll be lounging in the back of their Daimler, drinking champagne?"

Emma laughed. "Well, since he's the only one who doesn't have any work to do, I don't see why not."

David made a quick, pithy speech, welcoming everyone, reiterating the importance of the message, and thanking the volunteers, then started his wrap-up.

"The organizers already have all our cars nicely lined up and in about ten minutes will start to distribute the rally sheets. Navs, remember to check the gimmick list of things to look for and photograph, and submit them at the end of each day to the email address at the top of the sheet. The contestants who find the most will be entered into a special prize-draw at the end of the rally. Good luck, remember the rules, and stay safe.

"I now declare Rally Round officially started!"

There were cheers, and a piper started playing what was, for the bagpipes, a jolly tune, as the contestants closest to the front of the line of cars began to move toward their vehicles. David and Josh got down from the stage and, to Val's surprise, started coming their way, hindered by people wanting to shake hands or take a quick snap.

"I'm going to run to the ladies'," Emma said, to Val's surprise, since they'd both gone not that long before.

"We have at least twenty-five minutes before we start," she said. "Don't you want to wait?"

But Emma was already on the move and just waved.

Val braced herself, as David and Josh came closer, putting on as bland a face as she could, even though just watching David walk was enough to make her heart race. He had a kind of smooth grace to his movements that reminded her very much of how he performed in bed, and the memories were enough to make her melt.

They were close enough that Griff recognized her and started prancing, tugging Josh along after him as he rushed to greet Val.

"Hello," she said, stooping down to hug him and having to avoid getting her face washed. "Aren't you dapper today?"

"Valerie." There was that laconic tone, but when she looked up his gaze was anything but lazy or cool. "How are you?"

"Very well, thank you," she said, trying for a similar intonation, as she straightened, feeling at a disadvantage stooped down in front of him. "And you?"

"The same. I don't think you've met my son. Josh, this is Mrs. Sterling. She's transplant-recipient coordinator at St. Agnes, in Liverpool. Val, my son, Dr. Josh Kennedy."

Josh grinned as he shook her hand. "Just Josh, Mrs. Sterling. There's only room for one Dr. Kennedy in this race, don't you think?"

She couldn't help smiling as she agreed. "Besides, you wouldn't want the responsibility that comes with the name here, would you?"

"No, I wouldn't," he replied with great emphasis, then said, "Dad, I'm going to take Griff for one last potty run before we head out."

"Thank you, son."

And before she was ready to be alone with David, even in such a crowd, it was just the two of them. He moved fractionally closer, and Val had to stop herself from reaching out to touch him, the craving making her knees weak.

"I've missed you," he said, his voice a low growl, all coolness disappearing, as though it had never been there. "Come to my room tonight."

"David..."

He held up his hand, stopping her refusal before it could even be properly formed.

"I've had to make alternate arrangements for my accommodation, because of Griff. I'm nowhere near the hotels where the rest of the competitors will be. No one—"

It was her turn to stop him, and she had to look away too, because she knew anyone with any sense would probably see the way she looked at him and realize she was crazy for him.

"Send me the address, and I'll see what happens. But Emma and I have adjoining rooms, so there's no guarantee I'll be able to slip away."

The five-minute warning horn blew, and she risked a glance at his face in time to see him nod and the mask come down over his expression again.

"See you later," was all he said, before he was striding off toward the start line, where the Daimler waited.

And thankfully she had enough time to get her breathing under control before Emma came back.

"All ready," Emma said, sounding a little breathless.

"Me too," Val replied, absently, watching Kaitlin Proctor walk back toward her car. She'd passed Val, trailing a camera operator, not long after David walked away, following in his path. "Did you bring those beads and jewelry findings you said you were going to?"

"I did," Emma said. "Why?"

"I want to make a pair of dangly earrings," Val replied. "Will you help me?"

Emma's eyebrows went up, but all she said was, "Sure. We'll do it during lunch, since I promised to have dinner with George and Tess tonight."

"Perfect," Val said as her heart gave a little leap.

Maybe she could get away to meet David after all.

The first day of the rally took them out of Edinburgh by a slightly circuitous route, then west for a short run, and south to Carlisle through Gretna Green.

David had been pleased with Josh's navigational skills and the fact his son had deciphered all of the gimmick clues on this leg: Arthur's Seat, dyed sheep at Bathgate, the Famous Blacksmiths Shop at Gretna Green, and a fragment of Hadrian's Wall being the most memorable. Each time they'd stopped to take the picture, they'd taken turns posing in the shot, many of which had a blurry Griff cutting a caper in them as well.

The members of the car club that had put them together had done a great job, but David had to remind himself not to say anything to Josh about the clues he remembered. His conscientious nature made him want Josh to figure them all out on his own.

Since they were the first car out, they were also the first into Carlisle, but David was pleased to see the turnout of other classic vehicles and people at the venue.

Carlisle was one of the smaller overnight stops, but even in those less populated urban areas, local hospitals, charities, and blood-collection services had set up all-day awareness events. The GDK Foundation support of those smaller events had been one of the many complaints Malcolm and his fellow malcontents had put forward, but David was proud of the wide support for the venture.

If it meant spending money to make them all a success, in his mind it was worth it.

Parking the Daimler, he took Griff for a potty walk in a convenient spot, doffing his hat to anyone who gave him funny looks.

He rolled his shoulders and stifled a yawn. The last week had been crazy, and he hadn't been sleeping well. In fact, he hadn't had a proper night's sleep since last Saturday, when he'd spent the night in Val's bed.

There was something going on with her, and he didn't know what exactly. There had been times, as they spoke on the phone, when he'd heard a strange note in her voice, but when he asked her if anything was wrong, she denied it.

If she weren't such a straightforward woman, he'd think she was lying.

Georgie had been like that too. No whining or complaining about every little thing, but a workmanlike ability to just get on with things, no matter what.

His stomach roiled at the thought, and he froze for a moment.

It was that trait that had led him to feel comfortable leaving Georgie at home alone the day she died, when she'd told him it was 'just a headache' and he should go to his all-day meeting.

Yet, it would be silly to compare the situations. Whatever was bothering Val could be anything and nothing to do with him at all. That didn't preclude him from wanting to know and trying to help her, if he could.

He'd asked if she'd be meeting her son in Newcastle, but up until then she still hadn't been sure, and he got the impression she didn't want to talk about it so let it drop. She was, he realized, very private, as well as having an exceptionally independent spirit. Not the type of person one pressed for information.

He knew that well, since he'd learned to keep his business to himself too. Or, as his mum used to say, "A closed mouth catches no flies."

Griff had finished doing his business and was nosing about in the grass. While David cleaned up after him, he chuckled, thinking how silly he must look, dressed in old-fashioned evening wear, picking up doggy poop. Once that chore was done, he checked his watch.

If they'd followed the directions and hadn't got lost or turned around, Val and Emma should be coming into the final checkpoint of the day any minute now.

As a few drops of rain pattered around him, he started back toward the hall where the booths had been set up, steeling himself for the meet and greet ahead. Josh came out the door just as David tossed the baggie in the garbage receptacle outside the main door, and the rain started coming down harder.

"There you are, Dad. I was beginning to think you and Griff had taken off in a swirl of your capes." Instead of holding the door open, Josh stepped out to stand under the small portico.

David chuckled, calling Griff to him, so as to get the pup out of the rain. He wasn't looking forward to sleeping in the room imbued with the scent of wet dog.

"You know Griff. He had to sniff the entire patch of grass before finding the perfect spot." He hovered by the door, glancing back into the parking lot. A fair number of cars had already come in, but there was no sign of the red Mini. "I was lucky he got done before the rain came down."

Just as he was thinking it was ridiculous to be lingering outside, he heard the unmistakable sound of a Mini's engine and glanced over his shoulder, relaxing as he recognized the car.

"I'm going in," Josh said abruptly. "Are you coming?"

"In a minute." Moved to honesty, he said, "I'm exhausted and dreading the meet and greet. I just want a few more minutes to decompress."

Josh gave him a sympathetic look but didn't

offer to stay. Instead, he said, "Give Griff to me, and I'll get the schmoozing started for you."

David smiled. "Thanks."

Then Josh pushed through the doors, Griff in tow, and David turned to see Val and Emma dashing through the rain toward him.

Emma stopped for a moment but then went in, and he was overjoyed when Val lingered outside with him.

"Tell me something," she said abruptly. "Is there a problem between your son and Emma?"

"Why?" he asked, not to be difficult but curious as to how she'd figured it out.

"Emma seems to be avoiding him at all costs. Just now, she sat in the car, fussing over something silly, but as soon as he turned to go inside, she got out."

There was no reason for her not to know. "They were an item, a few years ago. I'm not privy to why they broke up, but I guess it wasn't particularly amicable."

Pursing her lips, Val sent a glance toward the door.

"Well, for what it's worth, I don't think she's completely over it. If she were, she wouldn't care whether she saw him or not and wouldn't avoid him."

"Hmm," he said, thinking that might make life difficult for Emma in the near future, but keeping that thought to himself. As much as he liked the young woman in question, he had more important things on his mind. "Will I see you tonight?"

Heat stained her cheeks a rosy hue, but her sea-storm eyes never wavered, as she replied, "I suspect you will."

And, suddenly, he was ready to face the rest of the afternoon.

CHAPTER SEVENTEEN

THE FOLLOWING MORNING, Val dodged questions from Emma about her looking so tired by saying she never slept really well in a strange bed, which was patently untrue but satisfied her friend.

There was no way she was going to admit she'd been in David's private suite, having wild sex until after midnight! Nor would she admit that if she had the chance, she'd be going back for more.

David's lovemaking was definitely addictive, and knowing time was probably running out on their affair, she wanted to take full advantage while she could.

Leaving Carlisle, although Newcastle upon Tyne was almost directly east, the route took them south, dipping into the Lake District before sending them northeast again.

It took all of Val's concentration to keep them on track and figure out the gimmick clues, because the closer they got to Newcastle, the more antsy she got.

She'd called Liam several times over the last

couple of weeks, but he hadn't picked up the phone, finally forcing her to leave him a message, telling him she'd be in the city and would love to see him.

He hadn't responded.

If it hadn't been for seeing him posting on social media, she'd have been a lot more worried. As it was, she just had to accept he needed more time before he'd be willing to patch up their relationship.

His brother leaving home and then his grandmother's death had been hard on him. He'd never really settled in the village outside of Glasgow where they'd moved to take care of his grandmother. Originally, Val had thought to move her mum into the house in Newcastle where she and Des had lived. But once Des had put his foot down and issued his ultimatum, it had been easier to take the boys and move into Mum's cottage.

It had turned out to be a great choice for Val but far more difficult for her boys. When, after his gran died, Liam declared his intention to move back to Newcastle, Val had been devastated and left feeling like a failure.

With a bit of time and distance, she was inclined to think it might have been the best thing for her son. They'd both been grieving, in very different ways. He'd withdrawn, while she'd thrown herself into tying up her mum's affairs, preparing the cottage for sale, and searching for a new job. Surrounding herself with lists and tasks and motion when, now she thought, all Liam probably wanted was some peace and quiet and the ability not to have to be in her whirlwind.

He wasn't to know that storm had calmed. Hopefully, she thought, one day she'd be able to show him it had, and they could start to repair the holes in their relationship.

Until he was ready, though, she wouldn't force it.

As they drove into Newcastle, Emma said, "I'm starving. Those sandwiches and crisps they handed out at the lunch stop just barely kept me going, and I need something more filling before manning the booth."

Val nodded as she wrote up the last of her notes, before getting out at the designated spot and going to the marshal's tent to sign them in and submit their time sheet. As the marshal commended them on their almost flawless run, Val made a mental note to congratulate Emma on her driving. For someone who'd never run a rally before, she was doing marvelously.

As she was walking back to where Emma had parked, she could see a crowd standing near the door to the convention center and hear a band playing just outside the entrance. Unfortunately, she couldn't see what was going on, but as Emma came to join her and they moved that way, she suddenly heard a familiar voice calling, "Mum!"

Spinning around, she was already smiling with

tears in her eyes, as her son picked her up and gave her a huge bear hug.

"Liam!"

When David and Josh had reached Newcastle, they'd been greeted by the mayor and a band, neither of which was expected. And while Josh took Griff off to do his business, making sure the pup didn't pee on the mayor's leg, David had found himself—as Josh called it—schmoozing.

David was quite sure he'd gotten that expression from his grandmother, since it sounded like a word Cerise would use.

It was while he was taking a turn around the conference center with His Worship the Mayor that he saw Val with a young man who could only be her son and had to stare.

He'd never seen her so radiantly happy.

She was glowing, her smile so wide as they walked along, arm in arm, that David was dazzled and had to look away so as to be able to concentrate on what was being said around him. Then the mayor insisted on David joining him for lunch, which, as these things often did, stretched far into the afternoon, so that he missed the entire first day of the Newcastle event.

Later, when he was about to sit down to supper with Josh, he'd gotten a call from a GDK director, warning him Malcolm was up to his old tricks.

"The numbers have started coming in regarding new donor sign-ups, and he's already saying turnout is below the expected rate and the foundation will suffer irreparable harm."

"We've run two days," David replied. "And had three sign-up events. What kind of miracles would satisfy him?"

And while the director had sympathized, she'd also cautioned that David should tread carefully.

"He might not be popular or well-liked, but Malcolm is well-respected."

The call, on top of everything else the day had brought, had raised his stress levels exponentially.

The one bright spot in his evening had been a talk with his mother, who said she was planning a trip to England and would let him know as soon as the dates were finalized.

He might be fifty years old, but age hadn't dimmed the bond. Only misunderstanding and intolerance had, and he was determined to make it right.

After loading the pictures submitted by competitors and bystanders via email to the foundation webpage set up to chronicle the race, he sat back and rubbed his eyes. Earlier in the day he'd sent Val the address of the house where he was staying. Now, he really wanted to call, just to see how she was doing, but hesitated to disturb her, in case she was with her son.

Was it ridiculous to be disappointed that she hadn't invited him to meet Liam? Her imposed secrecy about their relationship was really beginning to chafe. Not being able to be with her in public, having to hide their relationship, was no longer as acceptable to him as it had been at the beginning. Surely she realized they were past that stage now?

But whenever he suggested going out together, to eat or anything else, she refused. It made him wonder where their relationship was going—if anywhere.

Shaking that thought off and refusing to dwell on it, he called to Griff and, clipping on his lead, took him out for a walk in a small, nearby green. As he was coming back, still thinking about the events of the day, his mother came back to mind, and he started singing her signature song, in a low voice so as not to disturb the neighbors.

As he turned into the path leading to the cottage, Griff gave a delighted woof and took off toward the door. Taken by surprise, David had the leash jerked from his hand and made a grab for it, but it was too late. Griff was already capering around Val, jumping, trying to lick her face, as she laughed and fended him off.

"Down, Griff," she said, still laughing. "Down, sir." She sent David a slanting, upward glance. "You know, if the medical career doesn't work out for you, you could always take up singing. You have a nice voice."

Bending, David snagged the leash, saying, "I didn't expect you."

Her laughter faded, and she gave him a long, searching look. "Is my being here inconvenient?"

"Not at all." God, he sounded stiff, even to his own ears. Opening the door, he waved her through. "Please, come in."

"Are you sure this is a good time?" she asked, as she preceded him inside.

"I am. And I'm sorry I sound surly. This hasn't been the best of days. Although I think it's safe to say it was a truly excellent one for you."

Her face lit up again, and she laughed. "You saw?"

"I did," he replied, unable to resist touching her, even if it was just to take her by the wrist and lead her over to the couch so they could sit side by side. "Just for a brief moment, before the mayor dragged me away for an overly long and hardly digestible lunch."

"I was hoping to introduce you to each other, but I didn't see you. He'll be back tomorrow, though, and he's promised to help at one of the tables. I was surprised at how much he knew about what we were doing. I guess when he heard I was driving in the rally, he took an interest."

Before he could answer, his phone rang, and he sighed. "Excuse me for a moment?"

She nodded, but some of the light in her eyes dimmed.

When he identified himself, a male voice said, "Dr. Kennedy, this is Dr. Hiroshi, from Synthe Laboratories."

"Yes, Dr. Hiroshi. What can I do for you?"

"I wanted to tell you that there is a potential match for one of your patients, Mr. Swelo Mdele. Of course, further testing will have to be done to confirm if they are truly compatible, but I saw the notice of urgency on the file and wanted to inform you right away."

David's heart rate had picked up at the name of his most ill patient, and he felt his stomach twist. "That's excellent news. Can you tell me where in the country the sample came from?"

"Edinburgh."

That was surprising. "Please send the information to the doctor of record as soon as possible, so the additional testing can begin immediately."

"I will, as soon as we hang up, but as you were listed as the consultant on the case, I wanted to contact you first."

"Thank you," he replied, keeping his voice level and professional, while inside he was yelling like a twelve-year-old boy at a drag race. "I appreciate it."

As soon as he hung up, he punched the air. "Yes!"

"What happened?" Val was watching him, amused.

"That desperately ill patient I told you about? There may be a match, out of Edinburgh, of all places."

"Oh, David, that's marvelous."

"It is. But even better, I can use this to show the board Rally Round is already showing signs of success."

She hesitated, then said, "Be careful that you're not placing too much store in this. You still have the HLA testing to do, as well as—"

"I know, but this will, at the very least, get Malcolm off my back and make it harder for him to have me voted out as CEO."

The look she gave him was long and level and made him frown.

"I know you're happy about it, and I don't blame you," she said slowly, one hand closing and opening rhythmically. "I'm just worried that if the match isn't viable after all, you'll be in a worse position than you are now."

He felt it then—that soul-deep fear of things potentially slipping from his fingers—although, in the moment, he wasn't sure what it was he feared losing. He needed her to see. To understand what it meant to him.

"I made a promise when I created GDK, to make it the best it could be and help as many people as it could. When I make a commitment,

I see it through to the end, and no matter what Malcolm or anyone else wants, that's what I plan to do."

She nodded, but there was something in her eyes that made a cold ball form in his stomach.

"Yes. I can see you doing just that, whether it's good for you or not."

He tried to parse out her words, could make no sense of them.

"What do you mean by that?"

She shook her head, a smile tipping the corners of her mouth, but it looked almost sad.

"I just mean that you're a fine, decent man. And that's one of the things I admire about you the most."

Then she leaned close and kissed him, as though to stop whatever he was planning to say from leaving his lips.

He let her have her way for a few moments and then broke away, knowing there was more to her words than she'd actually said.

"Tell me," he demanded.

But she just shook her head and reached for the side zipper of her dress, pulling it down to bare the smooth skin beneath.

"No more words, tonight," she replied, and her smile seemed to wobble, just a bit. "I don't want to talk anymore."

And when she slipped off her dress, then straddled his lap, David agreed whatever still had to be said could wait.

Making love with Val couldn't.

CHAPTER EIGHTEEN

VAL AWOKE THE morning of the second day in Newcastle heavy-eyed and inclined to stay in bed. Only the knowledge that Liam was coming back to spend the day with her at the convention center had her getting up.

She couldn't stomach breakfast, though, her insides roiling with the knowledge of what she had to do.

It had come to her the night before, when she heard David talk about commitment and his drive to fulfill promises made.

That was exactly the type of man he was— dedicated and focused on doing the right thing— and his being that way was exactly why she couldn't keep seeing him after the rally.

She'd woken up during the night, her hand numb and tingling, her arm aching. It had happened before, and she'd put it down to sleeping on it the wrong way, but last night she'd faced the truth.

There was no point in putting it off any longer. As soon as the rally was over, she had to go to the doctor, and that could mean she was about to find out she had MS.

And she had to put a stop to their affair before that happened because David was just the sort of man who would feel as though he had to stick with her, even if he really didn't want to.

Even if he didn't love her the way she was forced to admit to herself she loved him.

Putting on a happy face had never felt more difficult, but somehow she achieved it and got through the day, talking to people as they came to the transplant-info table she'd been assigned to.

Before lunchtime, she was pleased to see Liam interacting with the visitors too. He answered basic questions or referred people either to her or the doctor working with them if he didn't know the answer.

When David came over, she introduced them, but the excitement she'd felt at the thought of it happening the day before was gone, and she was glad when David was called away. She needed to distance herself from him, as best she could.

Emma had lunch with Val and Liam and struck up conversation with him, showing him pictures of the answers to the gimmick clues, while Val sat back and watched them chat and laugh together.

Later that evening, after Liam had gone home, as the two of them walked to a pub to get some supper, Emma said, "He's smart and a really nice lad. Do you think he'll go into medicine?"

If anyone had asked her that question a year ago, or even two, she'd have said no way, but now she just shrugged and said, "I don't know. He might, and I rather wish he would. He has the brains for it."

David had texted to say he had to meet with local dignitaries that evening and wasn't sure how late he'd be getting back to his room. Sad to miss even one night with him, with their time together so short, she'd also been somewhat relieved. It gave her a bit more time to gather her composure—and figure out what to say—before seeing him again.

The next morning, one of the documentary producers came to get Val for her stint navigating for Kaitlyn Proctor, who turned out to be the type who complained most of the time. A strange way for a comedian to behave, Val thought, but she suspected no one could spend their entire time smiling and joking.

"Who the hell came up with this route? Are you sure we're going the right way?" she groused as Val called out the turns.

"Yes," Val replied, trying to keep her growing annoyance out of her voice.

"This will have us ending up in the Pennines, which is just stupid. Probably some more of that gimmick nonsense," Kaitlyn grumbled. "Make sure you get the pictures when they come up."

"You'll have to slow down for that," she said mildly. "As it is, you're going too fast for the route instructions."

"Once we start filming, I'll slow down," Kaitlyn said, her lips tightening, as if even though Val was the navigator, she really didn't want any instruction from the passenger seat.

Then, when the camera came on, she was suddenly a completely different person.

Warm. Charming. Funny.

Val couldn't help comparing it to the two main facets of David's personality, except, of course, his was the opposite. To the world at large he was cool and distant, while to those he knew well, he was caring, lovable, passionate.

Val's interview seemed to go well, as she explained what she did at the hospital, spoke generally about the importance of transplantation, and gave some insight into how things had improved over the years.

Although having a hard time concentrating on the instructions, gimmick list, and interview questions all at once, somehow she got it done. Perry, the cameraman in the back seat, stopped filming.

"So what's your relationship with David Kennedy?"

Caught off guard by Kaitlyn's question, Val's

brain seized for an instant, before she could gather her composure.

"The left turn is coming up quickly, and then there's a right turn immediately afterwards," she said, glad to have those additional seconds to shore up her defenses. "And to answer your question, Dr. Kennedy and I have worked together."

From the corner of her eye, she saw Kaitlyn send her a sideways glance.

"That's it, eh? I thought maybe you knew each other better than that. There seems to be a certain...electricity when you're together."

The knot that formed in her stomach actually steadied her since it short-circuited her horrible habit of blushing when startled.

"No." She gave the word no emphasis but made her voice cool, happy with how composed she sounded, although her heart was pounding.

Kaitlyn lifted her hand off the gear lever and waved it in a careless gesture.

"I just wondered, having seen you two together quite a bit. And don't get me wrong, I wouldn't blame you if you made a play for him. Not only is he gorgeous, but think of all that lovely money he inherited just waiting to be spent on things that are far more fun than transplant research."

Val bit back the words rising to her lips and checked the paperwork, not wanting to encourage the odious woman.

Kaitlyn seemed completely unconcerned and

continued. "I just got rid of my fourth husband, but if I were going to make that mistake again, I'd be happy to make it with David Kennedy."

"You'd love to get your mitts on all that cash, wouldn't you, Kay?"

Perry's comment had Kaitlyn sending him a poisonous glance in the rearview mirror.

"Why not?" she asked. "His wife's been dead for twenty-plus years. If anyone's going to share in his fortune, why shouldn't it be me?" Val glanced over and intercepted another sideways glance. "Unless Mrs. Sterling wants to set the record straight and tell me he's off the market."

Val shrugged, feigning cool unconcern although she was seething inside. "I wouldn't know anything about Dr. Kennedy's status. Perhaps it's best to ask him?"

Kaitlyn laughed, the sound grating and unpleasant. "Maybe I will…later."

And thankfully they came to a gimmick clue, which meant filming for a few minutes and taking the requisite pictures, and by the time they got back into the car the subject was changed.

But Val was left with a sick feeling, deep inside.

She'd come to the decision to stop seeing him by the end of the rally, but apparently, she and David didn't have that time left. If someone like Kaitlyn Proctor had noticed the connection between them, it was time to end it, completely, before anyone else did.

Thankfully, they were to switch back to their original driving partners at the lunch stop, and it was a relief to bid farewell to Kaitlyn and Perry and go off to find Emma.

It took all her strength to pretend everything was fine for the rest of the day, when inside a maelstrom of emotions was battering her. By the time they got to Leeds, Val had a headache brewing but refused to give in to either the pain in her head or her heart.

There was no sign of David at the venue, and when she overheard someone saying the Lord Mayor of Leeds had taken him off somewhere, she was relieved.

Part of her just wanted to get the upcoming discussion over with, but mostly she never wanted it to happen at all.

When his text inviting her over that evening popped up while they were packing up the booth, her heart turned over, and ice trickled down her spine. Taking a deep breath, she replied she'd be by in about an hour, but her hands were shaking, making it hard to thumb in the letters on her phone. And it felt like the longest, most difficult hour of her life, as her feelings ran amok and tension wound her tighter and tighter.

By the time she found her way to his rental

apartment, her brain had shut down her emotional center, so it felt as if she were underwater.

He noticed as soon as she walked in, and she could feel his gaze on her as she bent to pet Griff, who whined gently and nudged her thigh, as if sensing that something was amiss.

"What is it?" he asked, in his forthright way. "What's happened?"

Her knees were shaking, so she eased past Griff to perch on the edge of a handy chair. The pup followed and placed his head in her lap.

"Kaitlyn Proctor knows there's something going on between us."

David relaxed, his shoulders dropped slightly, and he smiled, although his gaze remained watchful.

"Well, someone was bound to realize at some point. I think it means we should preempt any rumors and go public ourselves."

Val shook her head. "I don't. I think we should stop seeing each other."

David froze, just for an instant, then said, "That's a little drastic for the situation, don't you think?"

"No." She'd thought it through carefully—knew what she planned to say, so he wouldn't glean the truth. "Perhaps it seems that way to *you*, but for me it's the only solution. You're used to being a public figure, but I'm not. I have no interest in having my life put under a microscope, being dissected for other people's entertainment."

He took a step closer, then looked around, as though disoriented, before sinking down onto the couch. "Val, it's not as bad as all that. And everything I do is to help the foundation. To move it forward. I've worked too hard to make it a success and can't give it up, not even for you."

"I'm not asking you to." It was his Achilles' heel—this wonderful organization he'd built out of his pain and grief—and she felt guilty for using it this way. But she had to keep his attention focused there so he wouldn't ask questions she didn't want to answer. "I'm just saying that, while you wouldn't suffer from us being seen together, my life would be turned upside down."

"I don't see how."

He'd retreated into the cool, lazy tone she'd come to recognize—and despise—but this time she was glad of it, hoping it meant he accepted her words at face value.

"No one will be casting aspersions on you, but I'll be the gold digger, the mantrap. I'll be the subject of speculation and nasty rhetoric, both at work and in my private life."

"I don't think you're a gold digger. Doesn't my opinion outweigh everyone else's?"

"In a perfect world, of course it would, but this world is far from perfect, isn't it?" She held up her hand to stop him interrupting. "Not even a perfect world, but just the ordinary world, like the one I'm used to rather than the rarified one you live in. In that world, no one would give a damn who I was seeing, but in *this* world, I'll be stalked and talked about, especially after we inevitably break up."

He leaned back, and something hot and angry gleamed in his eyes.

"So you'll run away rather than give us a chance, just because of what people will say? Just because the work I do means I have to be in the spotlight and you don't like the glare? I thought maybe we'd gone beyond that—that we had further to go, together. I—"

He hesitated, then fell silent, his gaze hooded, not in desire now but as a shield. Val felt the barrier she'd built around her emotions cracking, and she knew she'd have to finish this and get away, before it broke completely.

"David." She made her voice firm and brisk, although it was one of the most difficult things she'd ever done. "We both know this wasn't meant to last. Why put myself through hell for a passing fancy? You have your life and your devotion to the foundation, and I have my own quiet, happy existence. Let's just agree to keep them separate, completely."

He could never know that she'd go through all of it, every ring of hell, to stay with him, but the pain once again radiating down her arm reminded her of just why she couldn't dare.

So she gave Griff one last scratch behind his pricked ear and stood up.

"Good-bye, David. I wish you well."

And although she told herself not to be surprised or hurt, she still was when all he said in return was, "Good-bye," as though it meant nothing at all to him that she was walking out of his life.

CHAPTER NINETEEN

DAVID SPENT THE rest of the evening and long into the night trying to come to terms with the implosion of his relationship with Val but could make little sense of it. Angry—hurt beyond belief—he tried to rationalize what she'd said, but everything was a jumble in his head.

She'd been completely clear, and although it hurt to admit it, he knew what she'd said was the truth.

There could be no reconciliation between his life and the one she wanted. Not when he'd invested everything he had and was into the foundation. When GDK stood as a tangible monument to what good he'd been able to do in his life, as well as offering him redemption for the things he'd messed up. Giving it up—any of it—was unthinkable.

And her privacy, so highly valued, would disappear in his world.

Even just a month ago, had a woman he'd seen a handful of times said she didn't want to continue with their relationship, he wouldn't have cared. Yet, when Val told him her decision, he'd wanted to beg for another chance, tell her anything she wanted to hear, just to get her to stay.

He'd almost told her he loved her but had bitten the words back.

Why make himself even more ridiculous in the face of her surety?

In the deepest recesses of his heart, he knew he'd do anything in his power to protect her from harm and to make right whatever wrongs she encountered through association with him. Just how he'd do so, he had no idea, but still it hurt that she didn't see that.

After a restless night, he put on a smiling face for Josh, and they made the run into Manchester, surprisingly without incident. For the first time he was glad to be in the first car, since once he'd taken care of Griff, he could plunge right in to being Dr. David Kennedy, CEO of GDK.

Somehow, for the first time in fifteen years, the mask didn't quite fit the way it usually did but felt askew.

Making his way around the room, he saw Emma but not Val and wondered if asking for her would be too obvious. He was still feeling too raw and hurt so he didn't, and he spent another restless night wondering how she was, and if she'd contact him or speak to him if he called.

It was juvenile, but there was nothing he could do to stop.

The following day she was at the information event in the morning, looking as wan and brittle as David felt, but she disappeared after lunch. Unable to take it anymore, he circled the room as casually as he could, until he was at the table Emma was manning. When she looked up and smiled, he tried to smile back but obviously didn't achieved a natural expression, as Emma sent him a sympathetic look.

His stomach clenched, but he relaxed as she said, "Poor David. You look absolutely exhausted, but it must be satisfying to see how well things are going."

"It is," he replied, trying to sound enthusiastic. "Your nav's skived off, has she?"

Emma shook her head, the corners of her lips turning down. "I sent her to rest. I've been worried about her for the last few days. She hasn't been herself."

"Oh?" He tried not to sound too interested, but his pulse rate kicked up. "What's been happening?"

Emma's frown deepened, as her brows contracted, causing lines above her nose. "I'm not sure. She's so private and independent she won't say, but I've caught her rubbing her arm periodically and clenching and relaxing her fingers as though they're numb. Then the last couple of days she's just seemed... I don't know...off."

Before he could ask anything more, he felt a touch on his shoulder and turned to find the journalist, Ryan Winterhauer, standing beside him.

"Can I have a word?" he asked after they'd exchanged greetings and he'd apologized for interrupting.

He led David off to one side, away from the crowd, where they wouldn't be easily overheard.

"Listen, I don't know if you've already been told, but there's a rumor going around about impropriety regarding the reports being issued by the foundation. Something about falsifying of numbers of attendees, sign-ups, and matches being made."

Stunned, David stared for a moment, an icy chasm opening up in his belly.

"What?"

Ryan nodded, pulling David farther back from the crowd.

"My producer just called to tell me and to ask my opinion on the report. I told her I thought it was hogwash. Attendance has been phenomenal, and while I've been working the kidney-disease info booth, we've had so many people sign up and give blood samples the lab's been hard-pressed to keep up. But is there anything you can tell me about a patient who was told there was a match, but it turned out not to be viable?"

Anger—red-hot and explosive—chased the chill from David's skin, and it took everything he had inside not to curse out loud. He had no doubt this was Malcolm, up to his old tricks, trying to put an end to the rally and wrest control of the foundation from David's hands.

But he'd gone too far this time, and he might very well end up destroying GDK entirely.

"I can't comment on the last point, but I can say no doctor, in my experience, tells a patient about a match until absolutely sure it's viable, so if that occurred, it must have been from an outside source." He reached for his phone, as he continued. "Excuse me, will you? I need to figure out what's going on before this gets out of hand."

"Of course. Let me know if you figure it out, will you?"

"If I can. But thank you for giving me the heads-up."

He was already outside the door talking to Rolly when what Emma had said about Val floated from the back of his mind to the forefront, and the pieces of the puzzle fell into place.

"I'll need to call you back," he said, cutting his PA off midsentence. "If you find out anything, let me know, but there's something I have to do."

Then he was heading back inside to find Emma.

* * *

Val heard the knock on her door and pulled herself off the bed to go see who it was. Seeing David standing in the corridor had her stepping back, as though perhaps he'd burst through the door.

Impossible to catch her breath or to subdue the wild rush of color to her face, and she considered not answering. But then he knocked again, harder this time, and she instinctively knew he didn't intend to stop until she let him in.

Inhaling as best she could, she held the air in her lungs for a moment before opening the door. He strode past her, then turned, and the stern expression on his face, the almost-feral glint in his eyes, made her legs weak.

"What are you doing here, David?" She wished she didn't feel so off-kilter—heart pounding, her palms sweating, untamable emotions rampaging through her system. It made her voice quaver, just when she needed it to be firm and decisive.

"You think you have MS, don't you?" It wasn't really a question but a statement, fierce and forthright. "And you didn't want me to know."

The air left her lungs, and the blood rushed from her head, making her dizzy. "What?" she finally gasped, still trying to maintain the lie, not wanting to have this conversation. "What?"

"The way you've been rubbing your arm, bending and flexing your fingers." He held up his hand, making a fist then opening it again, twice. "You're worried that what you're feeling are symptoms of MS."

She somehow made it to the bed, just before her legs gave out on her. "You don't know what you're talking about."

But her voice was weak—shaky—and she despised herself for it.

"I'm a doctor, Val, and although neurology isn't my specialty, I know MS can be genetic, and you told me your mother died from it. It's not hard to put two and two together."

He'd retreated into that cold, lazy way of talking, trying to mask his anger, and it sparked an answering ire in her.

"What difference does it make?" There. Now she sounded more like herself, and the heat firing out from her chest gave her much-needed strength. "You can think what you want, but it's still over between us, David."

He stepped back, as though her words physically struck him.

"Why? Because you don't want me to be around if you have MS? Or you think I wouldn't love you—take care of you—no matter what?"

You love me?

The words almost came out, but she pushed them back, not wanting to acknowledge them. In fact, after the first rush of pleasure, they made her angrier.

"No! Because I know you would, even if you didn't really want to. Because I refuse to become another project you take up and see through to the end."

She tried to keep her voice cool, controlled, but she couldn't. Not with every nerve in her body on fire with rage, and anguish, and the kind of love she'd never thought she'd find.

"Do you know what my mother said to me, when she was dying? She said, 'I'm so sorry you have to tend to me this way, Val, but I'm glad your dad isn't here to be burdened with me—to have to take care of me.' And I knew what she meant, David. I'm a nurse, and looking after her, seeing her like that, was the hardest thing I've ever done in my life. I'm *not* putting anyone I care about through that."

"Even if they want to be there for you? Even if *not* being there would be worse than taking care of you?"

"I don't want you." The rage built inside her, overtaking her, pouring out through the hateful, hurtful words. "I don't need you to take care of me. I don't need anyone. Just go away, David, and stop playing the noble knight intent on saving the helpless maiden who is actually neither helpless nor in need of saving."

For a long moment the only sound in the room was the rasp of her breath sawing in and out of her throat, but the sound of her heart pounding in her ears almost drowned it out.

Why won't he leave?

She wanted him to go because the anger that had sustained her was fading, fast, and if he stayed much longer she'd break down. Just dissolve into a crying mess, which was the last thing she wanted him to see.

Taking matters into her own hands, she heaved up off the bed and marched to the door. Flinging it open she stood there, silent, her chin up, daring him to say another word.

He didn't. Instead, he shook his head, his expression morphing from anger through pain to disbelief.

Then he left, and Val could let loose the tears of pain and loss she'd refused to shed in front of him.

Next morning, Val made sure to get to the venue just before the start of the day to avoid seeing David. Emma gave her a long, searching look, but Val didn't have the kind of personality that allowed self-indulgence for long. So thankfully, although she hadn't slept much, there was no evidence of her crying the afternoon before.

"Feeling a bit better?" Emma asked, as they prepared for the next leg of the race.

"I am," Val lied. "I think I'm getting too old

to be running rallies. It's completely messed up my sleep habits."

Emma snorted. "Sure, you are. You run rings around half of the younger volunteers, so try that line on someone else. Did David stop by to see you yesterday?"

Luckily, as she asked the question, the marshal waved them forward, and Emma had to concentrate on her driving, so she didn't see Val's instinctive reaction. So that's how he'd known where to find her.

"He did," she said mildly, having got herself under control. "Nice of him to check on me."

"I thought so too. By the way, I think there's some problems back in London, although I don't know exactly what kind. I heard a rumor that David's heading back to headquarters as soon as he gets to Birmingham."

Not wanting to hear anything more about David just then, Val changed the subject to the list of clues, and that discussion lasted until it was their time to start out.

Being mentally distracted, Val missed a clue, and they circled back quickly to take the requisite picture since, as Emma pointed out, they were on track to a perfect record. As they started off again, the Mini gave a cough and a buck, and Emma cursed under her breath.

"It's probably the gas line," she said. "Hopefully it'll get us to Birmingham."

Val half hoped it would break down, allowing her to go home rather than face seeing David every day for the next eight days, but knowing how keen Emma was to finish the race, she kept quiet.

But although it sputtered a few more times, they made it into the city before it decided to give up the ghost.

"I'm going to stop here, rather than try for the official parking area," Emma said, once they got to a likely spot, pulling the Mini over and out of the way of the other vehicles.

They both got out, and Emma was releasing the catch on the bonnet when a local news crew ran over to them, the reporter asking questions before he was even alongside them. Clearly annoyed, Emma waved him and his cameraman away, and Val stepped back, trying to get out of their path.

And then there was the sickening sensation of falling, and everything went dark.

CHAPTER TWENTY

DAVID MADE IT to the station in Birmingham just in time to catch the train that would get him into London in time for the emergency board meeting and dropped into his seat with a sigh.

Malcolm had finally had his way, and the night before David had got the notice for the meeting, giving him enough time to do some investigating as well as put out as many fires as he could. He'd had to call in favors from participating groups, asking them to forward all possible data, then get staff to work overtime, collating all they'd received, to prove there was no falsifying of numbers.

Someone had also leaked information anonymously about the Edinburgh match for Mr. Mdele, although thankfully not mentioning his name. They'd made it sound as though it had been touted to the patient as a certainty when it actually wasn't a good match at all. Just finding out the match was no longer considered viable was a blow. Having that fact plastered all over the newspapers and in the electronic media was almost as bad.

His main focus should have been on ensuring the survival of GDK, even if it meant sacrificing Rally Round, but his last encounter with Val insisted on intruding. Even now, while he knew he should be concentrating fully on the upcoming meeting, it was Val who invaded his thoughts and wouldn't leave.

He'd told her he loved her, and she hadn't even acknowledged it—perhaps didn't even believe it—but it was true, and he refused to believe there was nothing to be done to get her back.

She was the first—the only—woman who'd made him truly feel since Georgie died.

Brave, proud, independent Val, who'd rather face the specter of a degenerative disease on her own than lean on anyone else.

Rather than lean on him.

I'm not putting anyone I care about through that.

It was only those words that gave him any hope whatsoever. By admitting she cared about him, she'd left the door open, in his mind, even if it were just a sliver. It was up to him to try and figure out how to make it swing wide.

There'd also been a ring of truth to what she'd said to him the night in Leeds, about her not wanting to live in the glare of publicity that surrounded him almost daily.

At the time he'd thought she'd meant it generally, but with new insight he thought even then she'd been thinking about the MS. To be under constant scrutiny while fighting a disease that could cause a myriad of symptoms at any given time would be untenable.

He wouldn't want that. Not for her, and not for himself either.

It was time to face the truth: in Val he'd found a return to normalcy that had been missing from his life for over fifteen years.

Funny now to be able to see that he'd been constantly running, constantly busy, constantly striving so as to avoid the realities of his past. That while the foundation was definitely worthwhile, he'd used it not just to do good but as a smoke screen to hide behind and a barrier to keep everyone but Josh out.

Although he still believed in the foundation's mission, meeting Val had forced him, for the first time, to examine his true role in it. No, he wasn't the barker in the carnival Malcolm accused him of being, but neither was the older man completely wrong in his assessment. His father's death had put David in the middle of a circus, and he'd picked up his top hat, tails, and whip and had fashioned himself into the ringmaster.

Now, he could finally admit it wasn't healthy. Wasn't right. No longer made him happy or fulfilled.

If it ever had.

Yes, GDK was worth saving, but wasn't his life worth saving too? And, most importantly, wasn't his relationship with Val worth everything else? Even if she ultimately rejected him, she deserved to know the truth: that what they'd found together in the moonlight was more important to him than anything.

At peace in a way he hadn't felt for more than seventeen years, he sat for a while, formulating a plan. The he took out his phone and called Val. When she didn't answer, he wasn't really surprised so he left her a message, hoping she'd call him back.

Then he made one more call, resolved to come clean so as to start anew, whether with or without Val.

Although, he hoped to God it would be with, since he didn't think he'd be whole, ever again, without her.

On the morning after the run to Birmingham, Val woke up disoriented, wondering where on earth she was—why the sounds she was hearing were so familiar and yet completely out of context.

Then she remembered.

She was in the hospital, after tripping over a cable, falling, and hitting her head. She'd been kept overnight for observation, making sure she didn't have a concussion.

As it turned out she did have a mild one, but the doctor had reassured her she'd be released today. He'd also said she was cleared to go back to the rally if she wanted to. Luckily for her, her attending physician was a rally buff, so he knew what a TSD rally was about and that it didn't involve high speeds and crazy antics. It also helped that the next leg didn't start until the following day, so she could rest.

Sitting up in the bed, she glanced over at her phone, tempted to pick it up and listen to the recording of David saying "Please call me" again.

Yet, she didn't.

Nor did she call, as he'd asked.

She'd said all she'd meant to, and even though she loved him, she couldn't give in to the urge to backtrack and tell him she'd changed her mind.

If things were different, she'd gladly deal with the whirlwind, high-flying life he lived, although it was so far outside of her experience she'd be terrified. The cool, drawling society figure most people saw wasn't attractive to her. Instead, she yearned for the solid, gentle, passionate man she'd come to know and love.

Her moonlight lover.

Accepting that none of it was to be broke her heart and made her feel emotions she hadn't known existed inside her. He'd shattered her self-image, showing her she wasn't only the prosaic, practical, mousy woman she'd thought she was, revealing the joyful, sensual side she'd forgotten she had.

She couldn't regret knowing him, though. He'd come into her life when she was unable to see her way ahead and taken her on a lovely, fairy-tale journey at a time when she'd thought romance of any type behind her.

If nothing else, meeting David had shown her there were still adventures to be sought and had given her the strength to seek them.

"Good morning." A nurse's aide bustled in and set down a tray on the lap table.

"Good morning."

"I brought you some breakfast, and Nurse Sawyer says the doctor will be by to see you about the results of your scan first thing this morning."

"Thank you," she said, as her heart gave a kick in reaction to her words.

"Oh, you're one of the rally people, aren't you?"

"I am."

"Well, that hunky Dr. Kennedy is on TV, giving an interview about it."

Before the young woman left the room, Val had the remote in hand and the set turned on. Flipping through the channels, she found the right one, just in time to hear a journalist asking David a question.

"...out who was behind the story that cast aspersions on the validity of the rally?"

"We have, and the matter has been dealt with, which is all I can say, legally."

"So where do you go from here? Will the rally continue?"

"Of course. Everyone involved has put in too much work for us to stop. Besides, I've received statistics showing on average a twenty-five-percent increase in donor sign-ups, testing, and blood donations after only the first week. I think that makes all the work worthwhile, don't you?"

"And what about your future with the foundation, Dr. Kennedy? One of the rumors was that you would be stepping down, not just as chairman and CEO but from the board completely."

David smiled, and Val realized there was something very different about him. He looked more relaxed. More comfortable in his skin.

"I'm afraid that was wishful thinking on some people's part. I'll be remaining on the board, but in a lesser capacity."

"Can you tell us why? Are you being forced out of the leadership position?"

"No. It's a decision based on the fact I'd like to go back to a more normal life. Recently I've been reminded of what's important to me, personally—things like moonlight, and vegetable gardens, and especially the people I love. Even when things are difficult or painful, I know those people mean more to me than anything, but I can't be the man they need me to be if I put the foundation rather than my personal life first."

Val's breath stuck in her chest, as his words struck home, knowing—believing without a doubt—he was telling her he wanted to be with her, no matter what.

She watched the rest of the interview in a daze, shocked to hear him talk about those horrible years, starting with his wife dying and ending with the court case. He even talked about the pain of never knowing his father and the Dupuytren's contracture and how it had put an end to his surgical career.

It was like watching someone fling wide the doors of a previously locked closet and take everything out and then repack it one item at a time, so all the contents were visible.

By the time the interviewer thanked him and the theme music was playing, Val was crying, and she knew it was combination of fear and hope and happiness for David.

Because he'd made a fresh start, and she knew he'd be happier for it.

But listening to him talk about Georgie, and how her death had affected him, could she really take the chance of putting him through a similar situation again?

She really wasn't sure she wanted to, because she loved him.

CHAPTER TWENTY-ONE

WHEN DAVID LEFT the studio and turned his phone back on, there must have been a hundred or more messages, but none from the one person he wanted to hear from.

Val.

Maybe she hadn't seen the interview, although he'd suggested to Josh that they inform all the participants in the rally that it would be on. Or perhaps she didn't care the way he'd hoped.

He was being driven back to the station when his phone rang. His heart turned over but then settled down again when he saw it was Josh.

"Dad…" Josh's voice cracked, and David heard him clear his throat before he continued. "Dad, that was one of the bravest things I think I've ever seen anyone do."

"Thank you, son," he replied, his heart full. "I'm heading back to the train station now, so I should be in Birmingham in two and a half hours."

They chatted for a few more minutes and then rang off.

He obsessively checked his phone every two minutes all the way to the station and then on the train. Less than an hour away from Birmingham, he got a call from a number he recognized. It was St. Agnes Hospital to inform him a donor had been found for Tamika Watkiss.

"We called Mrs. Sterling, and she said she'll be on her way back as soon as she can get a train from Birmingham."

"I will be too," he said, going on to explain where he was.

As soon as he hung up with them, finally Val called.

"David?" She sounded tentative. "Did you hear from St. Agnes?"

"I did. I'm heading toward Birmingham now. Where are you?"

"I'm going online and buying my ticket to Liverpool. Should I get one for you on the same train?"

He noticed she hadn't answered his question about her location. If she wanted to play it cool, he would too, although his heart was hammering, and his palms were damp.

"Yes, as long as it doesn't leave for at least fifty minutes."

"All right. I'll see you at the station then."

He wanted to tell her he loved her, but he bit his

tongue. If she didn't want to hear it, he wouldn't force the issue, even though it would break his heart all over again.

The rest of the trip into Birmingham, he was on pins and needles. Val emailed his ticket to him and told him she was on her way to the station, and he called Josh to let him know what was happening.

"I'll take care of everything, Dad. Don't worry."

And bearing in mind his new resolution to delegate more, he simply said, "Okay, son. Thanks, and let me know if you need any help with anything."

As the train drew into Birmingham, David's heart was beating so hard he felt slightly ill, and when he stepped onto the platform and saw Val waiting, he froze in fear for an instant.

Then he got closer and realized the tip of her nose was pink, and her eyelids were puffy, and he didn't know what that meant, but knew he couldn't go another step without finding out.

Stopping a foot away from her, he said, "You've been crying. Why?"

"I saw your interview. What did you mean, about moonlight and veggie patches?"

Hardly able to get his lungs to work properly, he replied, "That I love you, and I want to be with you. I needed to make sure you know you already have my heart, whether you want it or not, and that I'm yours, no matter what the future may hold, for either of us."

She didn't reply. Not with words, anyway. But since she was in his arms and kissing him as though she never wanted to stop, he didn't mind.

Not one little bit.

Then they had to make a dash for their train, but there were still things David needed to say, and once they were in their seats and had caught their breath, he took her hand.

"I don't care if you have MS. We'll deal with whatever comes, together, if you're willing. Even though I didn't realize my heart was still broken, even after all these years, you've healed it, and I love you more than I thought I could ever love again."

Her gaze was intent on his face, her eyes more blue than green just then, and so beautiful he felt their impact straight through to his soul.

"Meeting you has made me realize life, no matter how tenuous or frightening, is worth living to the fullest," she said softly. "Thankfully, I don't have MS right now, although that doesn't mean I mightn't get it later. I found out there were no lesions on my brain when they scanned it in the hospital yesterday to make sure my concussion wasn't too bad."

He leaned back to look at her, his heart suddenly faltering. "What concussion?"

She explained about tripping and getting

knocked out at the finish in Birmingham, ending with, "At the hospital I explained to the doctor what had been happening, and he suggested that, since they'd be scanning my brain anyway, they'd check for lesions at the same time. He also said he thought the arm pain and tingling in my hands may be a pinched nerve, so I'll get it looked at by my GP."

He was so thankful that for a moment he couldn't even speak, just hold her close and absorb the sensation of her body against his.

When he finally found his voice again, he said, "I'll never desert you, love. Not in this life, or the next. No matter what comes. Will you marry me, Val? I want to live with you for the rest of our lives and share every moment we can together, from now until forever."

"By sun and by moonlight," she said. "Yes, darling. Yes."

* * * * *